Fire Whisperer
&
Circle of Souls

Two Novellas of the Supernatural

Best Wishes,
Lynn Clark

Also by Lynn L. Clark

The Home Child

Fire Whisperer
&
Circle of Souls

Two Novellas of the Supernatural

Lynn L. Clark

The Plaid Raccoon Press

2015

ISBN: 978-1-927884-05-8
eBook ISBN: 978-1-927884-06-5

Front cover photographs: Ron Chapple and cyrano23/ Thinkstock
Back cover photograph: DrPAS/Thinkstock
Cover design by Michael J. McCann

www.theplaidraccoonpress.com

Fire Whisperer

For Mike and Tim,
the two loves of my life.

1

If she were to describe to an outsider how she viewed her life, Keva would say that it had been surgically split in two. There was the *before* time and the *after* time. The demarcation line between the two was THE FIRE—she always thought of it in capital letters—which had altered the course of her life.

Her memories concerning the fire itself were vague. She had a hazy recollection of lying on a stretcher while an alarm blared in the background. There had been a paramedic hovering over her and exclaiming with relief when she opened her eyes.

She remembered nothing else until she woke up in the hospital, her lungs painfully seared from smoke inhalation. She had shown steady progress in her physical healing. Her mental state was another matter. For the past ten years, she had tried to take back her life. She was still in therapy after all this time.

The hallucinations had begun after the fire. She would awaken during the night to see someone sitting on her bed or she would peer into the mirror and see someone else's image superimposed on hers. The images were blurred so that she never knew whose face she was looking at.

Then the voice in her head began—a constant murmur. Most of the words she didn't understand, because they seemed to be in a foreign language. The sounds were guttural, and she thought it might be Latin.

She felt detached from herself, as if she were a different person. The initial diagnosis was schizophrenia, and at first Keva had been hospitalized in a psychiatric facility and placed on heavy medication.

The risperidone she'd been prescribed had seemingly improved her mental health and after a year, her doctors thought Keva was showing signs of being able to function on her own. She progressed from in-patient to out-patient status. To control her anxiety and depression, her current therapist had recommended daily exercise and had also suggested some relaxation and coping techniques.

In reality, the voice in Keva's head still existed, but she had learned to tune it out. Her hallucinations still occurred, although less frequently, and she never spoke of them again to anyone, least of all to her therapist.

She had built a life of sorts for herself, studying photography at Algonquin College in Ottawa and working at a photography studio as an assistant and general gofer. The pay wasn't great, but it covered her rent and groceries. When she dared to think of the future, she dreamed of having her own studio.

Keva lived in an ancient apartment building in downtown Ottawa kitty-corner to a shopping centre. The building was so old that it had once been heated by steam from water-filled radiators. The landlord had finally installed baseboard heaters the previous year. She had lived there almost seven years. The rent was reasonable—or as reasonable as rent got in Ottawa—and the downtown location meant that she didn't need to have a car. What wasn't within walking distance she reached by bus or taxi.

She was twenty-seven years old now. The tenth anniversary of the fire was approaching. It was a constant presence in her thoughts—one that she could not push aside.

Keva cleared a spot on the moisture-ridden window of her living room and looked outside at the falling rain that shone in the glare of the streetlights. A young couple waiting at the crosswalk embraced and then ran arm-in-arm across the street, laughing, when the traffic light changed.

They're happy. She repeated the word several times in her head, but it seemed like an alien concept to her.

****

With a start, Keva realized she was still at the window of her apartment, seeing nothing outside as her fingers traced circle after circle in the moisture. These reveries had increased in frequency lately with the anniversary looming. The start of the ill-fated vacation which led to the fire was the very last time she'd felt optimistic about anything in her life.

Keva closed the curtain and began preparing for bed. She shook her head angrily at herself for being so careless as to stand that long in front of the window. She felt vulnerable to the gaze of passers-by and knew this was a high-risk building for break-ins. Half the time the front door of the building wasn't even locked, but instead was propped open with a brick to accommodate visitors to other apartments.

As she finally drifted off to sleep, paralysis overtook her. She saw flames in her room, but her muscles were locked and she could not escape. She struggled desperately to wake up and initially thought she had succeeded in doing so because the flames had disappeared.

But then she saw a young woman in her mid-twenties with flowing dark hair. The woman tried to speak to Keva, but no words came out at first.

Finally, after several aborted attempts to speak, the young woman said: "You are not who you think you are."

And then the flames reappeared and consumed her.

The Before Time

2

Keva was the only child of Myra and Gerald Tait, who'd met as undergraduates at the University of Ottawa and married when they were too young and too naïve to understand the commitments that marriage required.

Myra earned a degree in chemistry and started working at the National Research Council while Gerald finished his degrees in biology. Once he had obtained his PhD through the Ottawa-Carleton Institute of Biology, he succeeded in obtaining a position at the University of Ottawa. His early years were spent in research and publication while he established himself and rode the tenure track.

For her part, Myra wanted nothing to do with her husband's colleagues and their spouses. The few events she did attend at the university did not go well for her. She inevitably insulted someone by being too outspoken, and the Taits usually left these events early. It was not that she was unsupportive of her husband, but simply that she wanted validation of her own life and career.

Myra and Gerald Tait had been married eight

years when their daughter was born. They'd chosen "Kevin" as a boy's name in the event they had a son. When their daughter arrived, they couldn't agree on a girl's name, and decided to use a variant of the name Kevin. So *Keva* became their daughter's name. Later, Keva would remark to her psychiatrists that even her name didn't really belong to her.

Myra lost her job at the NRC due to cutbacks shortly before Keva's birth and was at home full time with her new daughter. For the first few years it worked out well for both mother and daughter. Keva would later tell her therapists that her mother was very attentive and lots of fun to be with. They were like best friends, always playing dress-up, being theatrical, and giggling with delight at some silly joke.

By contrast her father spent more and more time at the university. The young Keva loved him dearly, but didn't understand his constant absences.

Things began to unravel when Keva entered primary school. Her mother decided it was time to go back to work, but couldn't find anything other than what she viewed as menial labour. She became progressively more bitter as she stayed at home alone—dabbling in painting and photography—while her husband continued to excel in his career and became head of his department.

Myra's drinking started innocently enough—a glass or two of wine at dinner—but it soon spiralled out of control because of her unhappiness. She was also being heavily sedated with anti-depressants by her doctor.

The arguments between Keva's parents started after her mother's drinking got out of hand. They'd scream at each other in the living room while the young Keva cowered in bed and covered her head with a pillow to muffle the sound. And there were always crashes. Her mother threw things when she was angry, and when Gerald Tait tried to calm his wife, he always used a patronizing tone that only made her more infuriated.

It was like this for several years. Keva buried herself in her school work and was too ashamed to bring home any of her friends—what few she had—because of her mother's drinking.

And, then, it was as if a miracle happened. Myra Tait decided on her own to join AA. She was able to straighten herself out and find a job with a private research lab. Her new job seemed to brighten her perspective on everything.

The Taits' relationship, however, still remained a troubled one. Gerald kept putting in long hours at the university and when he was home, he found papers to grade or some other excuse to lock himself away in his study.

When Keva was seventeen years old and ready to enter university in the fall, her father booked two weeks' vacation in the Thousand Islands area. It was a fairly short drive away from Ottawa, but they had never taken the time to visit it.

Gerald and his wife still had feelings for each other, and he saw this as a last-ditch effort to save his marriage and keep his family together.

3

To her relief, the seventeen-year-old Keva noted that both of her parents seemed more relaxed on their drive to Gananoque, as if they were genuinely looking forward to this vacation. She turned her attention to the pamphlet in her hand, reading parts of it aloud to her parents:

> *Welcome to the beautiful Thousand Islands with more than 1,800 islands along our Canada-United States border. This area is a nature-lover's paradise with greenery as far as the eye can see...*
>
> *Kick back and relax; take a walk or a hike in our national park; or enjoy a ferry trip to visit ancient castles...*

"We have to see the castles for sure," Keva announced to her parents, "and go for long walks and take lots and lots of pictures." She had been an avid photographer since the age of fifteen.

"We'll have lots of time, honey, to do those

things," her father assured her. "But once we get there, how about we just relax and scout out the hotel, maybe take a swim in the pool—it looks beautiful from the pictures—and then enjoy a nice dinner."

"That sounds great," her mother chimed in. "If we can believe the online reviews, it's supposed to be a wonderful hotel with great food."

"It better be at the price I'm paying," her father groused good-naturedly.

As they drove up to the entrance of the hotel, Keva noted with pleasure that it was new and huge and looked inviting. She had seldom been away from home and was really looking forward to this experience. Her parents had even booked an adjoining suite for her to ensure her (and their) privacy.

The doorman helped them with their luggage and then called a valet to park their car. While her parents were at the registration desk, Keva walked the lobby and grabbed a handful of tourist brochures. To her delight, there were local cruises, as well as live theatre at the nearby playhouse. She also noted there was a casino, and she began plotting how to convince her parents to go there for an evening. It would be something they'd never done before. She wanted so much to see them make a new start.

The first week was wonderful. Their room had a beautiful view; the food in the hotel restaurant was great; and they had already gone on several short cruises and nature walks. It was shaping up to be a great vacation.

And they still had another week to go.

4

It was early morning, and the sun shone through a slight gap in the curtains. Gerald Tait watched his wife sleeping beside him and tried to recall what it was like in the early years of their marriage. The world had seemed full of opportunities then. That was before his struggle for acceptance at the university, the competition for dwindling research grants, and the constant pressure to publish articles in the finite number of academic journals available to him in order to get tenure.

Somewhere along the way, he'd let his wife and daughter slip further and further away while he buried himself in his work, not wanting to admit how much life disappointed him. But more than that, he'd disappointed himself. He'd met one of his female colleagues at an out-of-town conference, and they'd begun an affair. It was now in its second year. They often met at her house after classes were finished for the day.

He shook his head. *What was that line from the old Eagles song Myra used to hum? Something about being so far gone that you feel like a fool.*

He wanted to end the affair and make a new start with his wife, but he continued to drift along with the status quo because that had always been the easiest path for him.

5

Myra lay beside her husband, aware of his gaze, but feigning sleep because it seemed that she never knew what to say to him to bridge the chasm between them. In the early years of their marriage, she'd assumed there was nothing they couldn't handle together. But that wasn't the case any more. She felt almost superfluous.

Maybe this vacation will help us get back to what we used to be together. Gerald definitely seems more relaxed here, and it's the most time we've spent together as a family since I can remember.

Keva entered their room from her adjoining suite, opening the curtains and flooding the room with sunlight.

"Rise and shine, parents. We have a busy day ahead of us. We're going exploring today, remember? And then we have the play tonight."

The day passed quickly as they hiked the nature trails in the park, Myra and Gerald trying valiantly to keep up with their daughter. They returned for lunch and then took a dip in the pool. Myra and Gerald relaxed in lounge chairs afterward while

Keva took her camera outside to take photos of the water birds that gracefully circled the islands. When she finally returned—excited about all her great shots—it was time to get ready for the theatre. They were going to see a Restoration comedy that Keva had read as part of her high school English curriculum.

As they entered the playhouse, Myra heard a distinctive voice, which she recognized as belonging to the wife of one of Gerald's colleagues at the university. They had exchanged small talk at a faculty party. Myra turned to comment to her husband, but saw that he and Keva were already moving toward the ticket-taker. She hurried to catch up with them.

During the first intermission, Myra went to the washroom while Gerald and Keva sauntered over to the refreshment stand. She was still in one of the cubicles when she heard the voice of the woman she'd recognized earlier in the lobby. The woman— she thought her name was Vera—was speaking to a companion, her tone excited, no doubt signalling that she was about to reveal some particularly juicy piece of gossip.

"I see Gerald Tait is here with that snooty wife of his. I met her at a faculty party. You'd think he'd have asked her for a divorce by now. He's always with that other professor—Mary Connors—and it's an open secret that they're having an affair—"

Myra didn't hear the rest of it. She was too

shocked and hurt. She remained in the cubicle until the women left, and then found Gerald and Keva and pleaded a headache. She hurried back to the hotel.

Without even thinking of the consequences—she had been sober for eight years—Myra entered the hotel bar and ordered bourbon. She had four drinks before heading up to her room.

Alcohol always intensified Myra's unhappiness and made her temper run ragged. She was already in a rage when she entered the room and slammed the door behind her. She'd bought a pack of cigarettes at the bar, an indulgence she allowed herself from time to time. She threw her purse on the bed, retrieved a bottle from the mini-bar, and managed to locate an ashtray. She lit the first cigarette from the pack and collapsed on the bed, her drink beside her on the nightstand.

Christ, what an idiot I am. I should have known what was going on with him. I thought he was just preoccupied with his work—

Suddenly she could hear voices outside the door. Gerald and Keva were returning from the play. Myra barely had time to hide her drink before the door opened.

"Hi, Mom. Sorry you had to leave early. Is your head any better?" Keva asked.

"I'm feeling better, thanks. Did you enjoy the play?" Myra responded, avoiding eye contact with her husband.

"It was fun, Mom," Keva said as she made her way to her adjoining room. "Thanks for getting the tickets for us. I'm tired though. I think the hike today did me in. I'll see you both in the morning. Sweet dreams."

But I forget how to dream, Myra thought.

6

Keva awoke around 11 PM to the sound of loud voices coming from her parents' room. They hadn't argued like this since her mom had stopped drinking. She couldn't make out their words, but she knew her mother was very angry. Her father's voice was more subdued, as if he were pleading with his wife.

Suddenly she heard a loud crash. Alarmed, she went to the connecting door to listen, trying to work up the courage to enter her parents' room. She had her hand on the knob—

Keva had no further memory of the event until she woke up on the gurney with the paramedic peering anxiously over her.

The After Time

7

Keva awoke that May morning feeling groggy and disoriented after last night's sleep paralysis. She was running late for work and had forgotten to make her lunch, thinking of it belatedly as she hurried to the studio where she worked. She hoped that she had enough money in her purse to duck out for a quick sandwich.

She flicked on the electric OPEN sign as she entered the studio. It seemed that every small business on the street had one now that Costco was selling them. She raised the blind on the door and began to prepare the till for the day. Almost everyone paid by debit or credit card, but the owner, Arthur Selken, still liked to keep money on hand in case someone actually paid in cash.

The morning went quickly. There were three engagement photo sessions, and each of the couples lingered behind to look at sample wedding albums.

Around noon she called out to Arthur, "I'm starving, and I forgot my lunch. Is it okay if I duck out for some?"

"No problem," he replied absent-mindedly as he arranged his equipment for his afternoon appointments.

She walked to a nearby Tim Hortons to pick up a sandwich, thinking she would bring it back to the studio to eat. There was a long line-up—when wasn't there a long line-up here?—and she inadvertently jostled the arm of the man ahead of her. As he glanced back reflexively, she apologized to him.

"No harm done," he said, smiling at the small, red-haired woman behind him. He noticed that her curly hair seemed to have a mind of its own, sticking out at every angle from her face. "It's always so crowded in here. I don't know why I keep coming back. I guess it's the coffee. Maybe it really *is* super-addictive. I'm Matt, by the way. Matt Jensen," he said, offering her his hand.

"Keva Tait," she said, shaking his hand. "It's an unusual name, I know. It rhymes with *diva*, although I can assure you that I'm not one of those." She was babbling, not used to making small talk.

Matt turned back to the counter where the waitress was impatiently beckoning him to come forward. Embarrassed, he gave his order and then moved down the counter to wait for it to be filled.

Keva ordered her meal, asking for takeout, and then hurriedly returned to the studio. On the way there, she kicked herself mentally for having talked to a complete stranger.

Didn't your mother and father teach you

anything?

But he seemed nice enough.

Sure he did. A real charmer, just like Ted Bundy, the serial killer.

Back and forth she went with her mental dialogue, finally admitting that she'd found him attractive and hoped to see him again.

Later that evening when Keva was back in her apartment, she googled his name, getting about twelve hits. Assuming that he worked nearby, she was able to eliminate most of the entries and was down to two possibilities. One worked in a nearby law firm on Slater Street. The other was an employee of the federal government. Neither had Facebook accounts where she could check out their photos.

Okay, enough of this nonsense. Time for bed.

Keva realized she was dreading the prospect of going to sleep because of the nightmares she'd been suffering lately. And as she finally drifted off, she experienced the sleep paralysis of the previous night. Her muscles would not move no matter how urgently she willed them to.

The inevitable nightmare followed. The acrid smell of smoke, her body strapped to the stretcher. The paramedic hovering over her. And then the out-of-body experience of looking down from afar at her own body as it lay motionless there.

And a spectral figure standing behind the gurney, the young woman with flowing dark hair, who appeared to be whispering in her ear—

8

Keva sat in her therapist's waiting room, unaware that she was wringing her hands: a gesture she made when particularly stressed. She still dreaded these appointments even after all these years of therapy. Her illness had cost her dearly. She had withdrawn more and more into herself, fearing the reaction of others because she knew the stigma attached to mental illness was still very strong. If she wanted proof, she need look no further than the reaction of the cab drivers who brought her to these sessions. Today was no different. There was the usual awkward moment of silence after she'd given the address for the psychiatric hospital where her doctor's office was located. This was followed by the driver's furtive glances at her in his rear-view mirror. She never quite had the confidence to look up and meet those eyes in the mirror.

The receptionist called her name, and Keva entered her doctor's office. Dr. Finlayson was tall and gaunt. He reminded her of John Cleese, but without the sense of humour. She had learned not to attempt jokes with him because he regarded them as a form of deflection rather than as an attempt to lighten his sombre mood.

"Good morning, Keva," he said as she settled into the chair in front of his desk. The chair was upholstered and comfortable, and the walls of his office were painted in a light beige colour. The paintings that hung on them were of pastel flowers. The room had no doubt been carefully designed to provide a calming ambience. Psychology 101: create a soothing environment for the patient.

Although she hadn't intended to discuss the night terrors—as she thought of her sleep paralysis— Dr. Finlayson commented that she looked very tired.

"I'm having trouble sleeping," Keva admitted, "and when I fall asleep I'm experiencing paralysis. I've read up on the subject and I understand it's fairly common, but it's still very disturbing to me."

"How long has this been going on?"

"About three weeks now."

Dr. Finlayson began one of his elaborate explanations, which Keva always found annoying because they seemed designed to showcase his knowledge: "Well, you're right that paralysis in the transition between wakefulness and sleep is fairly common. About 40 per cent of the general population has experienced it, either when falling asleep or when trying to wake up. It's frightening, not only because of the inability to move or speak, but also because the paralysis is frequently accompanied by hallucinations."

Keva nodded dutifully, having read all of this in her research.

"Sleep paralysis can be triggered by depression and stress," he continued. "Are you feeling more anxious than usual these days, Keva? You should be using the breathing exercises I taught you to control your anxiety."

"I am, Dr. Finlayson, but the tenth anniversary of the fire is coming up. I expect that's triggering my stress."

"I see. Well, keep up the relaxation exercises. I'm also going to prescribe trazodone for you. It's a non-addictive sleeping aid. If the sleep disturbances continue, I'd recommend that you have the prescription filled. By the way, this might be a good time to reach out to your parents. They're no doubt mindful of the upcoming anniversary as well."

Keva nodded, anxious to be out of his office.

As she waited for the elevator, she pondered once again why she felt so uncomfortable in these sessions. When her condition was first diagnosed, she'd done a lot of research not only on the drugs being prescribed to her, but also on the treatment of women for mental illness. She knew that in the previous two centuries women were committed to asylums for having children out of wedlock, post-partum depression, and a number of so-called "women's illnesses." The old Rockwood lunatic asylum near Kingston, Ontario, had housed women in the stables until the former estate house was renovated to accommodate them.

Perhaps her feelings of discomfort arose from her belief that even in the twenty-first century, there was a lingering bias in the treatment of women for mental illness, especially among older, paternalistic psychiatrists like Dr. Finlayson.

On her most pessimistic days, such as today, she thought the field of psychiatry in general was still in the Dark Ages when it came to understanding the human mind and its illnesses. After all, it had been less than fifty years ago that lobotomies were routinely performed on patients in mental institutions.

She shivered involuntarily at the thought.

9

Gerald Tait folded his newspaper and took a last gulp of his morning coffee. He slid open the glass patio doors to his back deck and stepped outside to breathe the morning air. Even after all these years, he'd never quite become accustomed to the differences in climate between Ontario and British Columbia, where he now lived. Here it was early June, and most of the flowers were already in bloom. In Ottawa, there was still frost, and it had damaged many of the flowers at the yearly May tulip festival.

Gerald had fled Ottawa after the fire and was now teaching at Simon Fraser University. He and his wife had divorced, and he was living alone here. The fire had ended his relationship with Mary Connors as well as with his wife.

When Keva was hospitalized after the fire, Gerald had followed his daughter's progress closely. He'd paid for her apartment when she was released from the psychiatric facility until she had completed her studies at Algonquin College and found a job at Arthur Selken's studio. They corresponded sporadically through e-mail, but the years and distance had taken their toll on the father-daughter relationship. Keva was always polite and solicitous of his health, but there was none of the former spontaneity and love in their relationship.

Gerald Tait had yet to confront the tragedy that had torn apart his family. To confront it would be to accept his role in it.

10

After the fire, Myra Tait resumed her drinking and lost her job. Finally, two years after her divorce became final, she decided she wanted no more of Gerald's money to support her. She began once again to attend AA meetings and finally became sober. Presently, she rented a house in the west of Ottawa within walking distance of her current job.

Myra had visited her daughter each day in the hospital until her release, and they still met once a month for supper at Myra's home. She was cautiously optimistic that one day Keva would forgive her.

She knew that she could never forgive herself.

11

Keva's sleep paralysis had continued, and she'd reluctantly decided to get the prescription for trazodone filled. Most nights the medication helped her, although she still continued to dream of the young, dark-haired woman and the fire.

Periodically, she would see an elderly lady sitting on her bed. There seemed to be a connection between the young woman of her dreams and the old woman of her hallucinations. As if they shared a common bond.

Her work at the photography shop engaged her thoughts during the day. Arthur had finally begun to share his workload with her. She was now doing most of the engagement pictures and assisting him on the wedding shoots.

On one particularly hectic day in late June, she decided to get lunch outside the shop for a break. As she was hurrying along the sidewalk, she heard someone call to her.

"Hey, where's the fire? Wait up."

The voice sounded vaguely familiar. She turned around to see the guy from Tim Hortons walking quickly behind her. Keva stopped to give him a chance to catch up.

"You're a hard woman to track down. I haven't seen you since that day at Tim Hortons. Remember me, Matt Jensen? It's Keva rhymes with diva, right?"

Keva nodded, still embarrassed by her last conversation with him. "I work in that photography shop," she gestured back in the general direction of the store. "This is our busiest time with summer weddings coming up and graduation photos to take. I usually bring my own lunch, but today I needed a break."

Great. I'm babbling again.

"Would you like to have lunch with me? There's a delicatessen around the corner that serves a great Montreal smoked meat sandwich."

"Sure," Keva said, with only a slight hesitation. "I'd enjoy that."

They managed to squeeze into the last empty counter seats and then placed their orders. While they were waiting, they talked. Matt explained that he worked as a paralegal in a Slater Street law office.

"I'm taking night classes and maybe in another ten years or so, at the rate I'm going, I'll get my law degree." He hesitated. "I hope you're not part of that 85 per cent or more of people who hate lawyers, by the way."

"I guess people hate lawyers until they really

need one, the same as with cops," Keva observed. "How long have you worked there?"

"Eight years now. It's not the most exciting job in the world. It's mainly handling estate documents and searching property titles, but I enjoy it. And it's a small firm, which also makes it nice. I don't have twenty or more lawyers coming at me with work. There are only two in the firm. What about you? How did you get into photography?"

"I started when I was fifteen. My parents bought me a camera, and I went around annoying everyone by constantly taking their pictures. I'm more of a gofer than a photographer at the shop, but at least my boss is finally trusting me with some of the work. It's taken him a long time to delegate stuff to me. I mean it's not like we're Karsh photographing Churchill. We just do wedding and graduation photography."

Their sandwiches arrived and they started eating, both conscious of the need to get back to work. When they'd finished, Matt asked Keva if she'd be willing to see him again. He saw a brief flash of alarm in her eyes, but she agreed to exchange phone numbers with him.

"I'll send business your way," Matt joked as he walked her back to the photography shop. "I have a ton of nieces and nephews who are getting married. I come from a big family."

Keva laughed and waved good-bye as she hurried inside, half-expecting a reprimand from

Arthur for being away too long. But he was busy with the phone and didn't even seem to notice her come in.

12

Later that evening, Keva was finding it very hard to stay awake. She watched some television, prepared tomorrow's lunch for work, and decided to do a quick wash in the basement of her apartment building.

As she balanced her clothes basket on one knee and opened the door to the laundry room, she heard the sound of the machines and saw that there was someone already in the room. She had her back to Keva, but turned around at the sound of the door opening and looked up.

Keva gasped involuntarily. This person was an older version of the young woman in her dreams.

"I'm sorry," the woman said. "I didn't mean to frighten you." She spoke with an accent that Keva couldn't place. "I'm Ada Schafer. I think we may have passed each other on the stairs from time to time. I live on the fourth floor."

"I'm Keva Tait, and my apartment's on the third floor. You look a lot like someone, um, I know. I guess that's why I was startled."

Trying to regain her composure, Keva continued

to chat as Ada folded her clothes and prepared to leave. She glanced up just as Ada was opening the laundry room door to go out. The woman was framed in the window beside the door, and the light from the dying sun cast an aura around her dark hair.

Keva had to shut her eyes. She could have sworn that Ada's hair was engulfed in flames.

****

When Keva returned to her apartment, she decided—against her better judgment—to call her father. There was a three-hour time difference, and he would probably just be getting back from the university.

Gerald Tait answered on the second ring, sounding worried. "Keva, is that you? Is everything okay?" He obviously had caller ID.

Keva forced a laugh. "I'm fine, Dad. I guess I don't call you often enough. I'm sorry if I alarmed you. I just called to chat and see how you're doing."

"That's great, Keva," her father said, although he suspected there was another reason for the call. "It's nice to hear your voice. Much better than e-mail. How have you been getting along?"

They talked for a few minutes about her job, and Keva mentioned that her boss Arthur Selken was finally delegating work to her.

"I've always suspected he was a bit jealous of

your photography skills, Keva, and thought you'd probably upstage him. It's good to hear that he's finally coming around and making use of your talent."

Eventually his daughter got to the point of her call. "Dad, with the tenth anniversary of the fire coming up, I've been thinking a lot about what happened. I know you and Mom have always told me that the fire was contained quickly and there were no casualties—just a few people like me treated for smoke inhalation—but are you sure of that? Is it possible that someone was more seriously injured and died afterward in the hospital?"

"Keva, we've been through this a hundred times. Your mother and I weren't lying to you. No one died in the fire—"

She interrupted him. "I know this will sound strange, Dad, but do you remember anything about the other guests in the rooms nearby? I keep having vague recollections"—this was the most plausible lie she could come up with—"of a young woman in her mid-twenties with long dark hair. Does that sound familiar to you? Is it possible she was one of the ones treated for smoke inhalation?"

"I vaguely remember there was a tour group there at the time. I think it was a youth orchestra. She could have been part of that group. But it doesn't mean anything, Keva, because no one was severely injured. I think you really have to move on, darling, if you're ever going to feel well again."

Keva talked a few more minutes with her father, and then ended the call, reassuring him that she wasn't obsessing about the fire. She knew that he didn't really believe that any more than she did.

As she prepared for bed, she thought once again of the woman in the laundry room, puzzling over the relationship between her and the young woman in her dreams.

Keva slept fairly well that night, awakening only once to find soot and ashes at the foot of her bed.

In the morning, all traces of them had disappeared.

13

The following day, Keva was showing sample wedding albums to a young couple. When they talked to each other, they spoke in another language. With a shock, she recognized the sounds of some of the words, although she didn't understand their meaning.

"Do you mind if I ask what language you're speaking? I'm sure I've heard it before."

The young woman looked embarrassed and apologized. "I didn't mean to be rude. I've attended English-speaking schools, but I'm still much more comfortable in my native language. I was speaking in German. It's the official language of Austria, where I was born."

"No need to apologize," Keva quickly reassured her, as the young woman explained that her parents spoke German exclusively at home, as did the parents of her fiancé.

When Keva returned home that evening, she looked at some journals she'd kept when first hospitalized. At her doctors' urging, she had tried to reproduce the words of the voice in her head:

the one that she'd managed, for the most part, to shut out. Recalling it was a painful process because it had nearly destroyed her sanity a decade ago. But somehow she was sure that it held the key to the identity of the woman in her dreams and to understanding what had happened when she was unconscious after the fire.

She'd written down the words phonetically in the journal. The spelling was incorrect so it took her several tries to come up with the actual German words—*sie sind nicht allein*—to search for online. When she found them, she stared numbly at the English translation: *You are not alone.*

She recalled the young woman of her dreams who'd told Keva that she was not the person she thought herself to be.

On an impulse, Keva entered new keywords in Google. She came across the following entry:

> *Many cultures share the belief that two souls can agree to exchange bodies. This experience is commonly referred to as a 'soul transference' or a 'walk-in,' and it is said to occur most frequently at the time of great trauma, such as when the host body suffers grievous injuries and seeks another home.*
>
> *In the case of a 'guest walk-in,' two souls will inhabit the same body.*

The new soul will bring comfort and counsel to the original soul of the host body when it is still debating whether to remain there or to leave its body permanently.

Keva shook her head. Soul transference might be a way of explaining the voice in her head and her hallucinations after the fire, but it made absolutely no sense to her. If no one had died in the fire, why would there be a need for a departing soul to enter her body? The whole idea seemed preposterous. Too New Agey to consider.

And yet she could not rid herself of the feeling that she'd lost her true identity in that fire.

Later that evening, Keva called her mother on the pretext of arranging their monthly visit and then steered the conversation toward the upcoming anniversary of the fire. "Mom, I know you don't like to talk about it, but I've been having vague recollections of someone who was hurt in the fire, and I think it's best to get it out in the open. Can you recall a young, dark-haired woman among the people sent to the hospital for smoke inhalation?"

There was a long pause at the other end. "The smoke only affected the rooms on either side of us. One room was thankfully empty at the time, and I don't recall who was in the other one."

"I think I remember a youth orchestra staying there," Keva dissembled, not wanting to identify her father as the source of this information. "Maybe its members checked in at the same time we did."

"There may have been, Keva, but I honestly don't—

"Wait a minute, yes, now I remember. When we went to the pool that first day, I realized I'd forgotten my earplugs. I went to the front desk to see if the hotel might have some for their guests. There was a group checking in. I remember because there was an organizer or tour guide who was translating for them."

14

Myra Tait sat in her living room after the call with her daughter had ended. It was like a form of torture for her, this constant rehashing of the events of the fire. But she would willingly go through this if it could somehow help her daughter.

One of the things that Keva never questioned her about was how the fire started. She suspected that her daughter didn't ask because she already knew the answer. Myra would relive that moment forever. Her husband attempting to placate her, telling her he would end his affair, trying to reason with her in that tone of voice she despised, pleading with her not to have anything else to drink.

In her mind she replayed what happened that night: her rage, the trajectory of the glass she had thrown as it hit the ashtray beside her bed, her husband shaking his head in disgust and sorrow and walking out of the hotel room, she herself collapsing in a chair, her thoughts thick with despair. She'd been too drunk to realize that a live cigarette had rolled onto the bedspread from the overturned ashtray. After dozing in the chair for a few seconds, she'd awoken to the sight of the bed engulfed in flames. The sprinkler in the room hadn't engaged immediately because of some type of malfunction, and the flames had spread quickly to the curtains. The room was thick with smoke.

And then she found her daughter, collapsed on the other side of the adjoining door.

It was a tableau that had played out in her mind in slow motion for ten years.

15

Matt Jensen had called Keva several times to arrange a date, but she'd put him off each time. In the past, none of her boy friends had stuck around long, after they'd learned of her mental illness. She didn't want to put herself through that heartache again. But when she'd finally run out of excuses, she agreed to meet him at the Italian restaurant in the shopping centre near her apartment. She generally didn't like being out alone at night, but in this case she could just walk across the street to get to the restaurant.

Because of the medication she was taking and her experience with her mother's alcoholism, Keva herself did not drink. It usually made for awkward conversation at meals, but when she was seated with Matt in the restaurant and had declined the beverage menu offered by the waiter, asking instead for ice water, Matt made no mention of it and simply requested the same.

"How are things going at your shop? Still swamped with work?" Matt asked, once the waiter had taken their orders.

"Yes, we've finished the grad photos for the most part, but we're fully booked for weddings until October. The recession doesn't seem to have hit the wedding industry so far," Keva replied. "What about you? How's your job going? It must be hard to work all day and then take classes at night. When do you have time to study and do assignments?"

Matt smiled. "Let's just say that I don't have a lot of down time. That's why I'm glad we're finally able to get together. I was afraid you'd tell me this time that you had to stay home and wash your hair. Then I would have known for sure that I'd bombed out."

Keva laughed, looking embarrassed. "I'm sorry. I'm just very cautious. I've had some pretty bad experiences in the past."

"No problem. I understand. I guess a lot of people hook up online nowadays, but I just never felt comfortable with that idea," Matt replied. "You have to come up with some spiffy way of selling yourself and that's not really my thing. 'Tall, dark, and average looking' doesn't really cut it. And besides, I prefer to talk to someone face-to-face."

16

Across the street, Ada Schafer sat in her apartment, staring vacantly at the living room wall. There was something about her meeting with that woman, Keva Tait, that still bothered her.

Why was she so shocked when she first saw me? And when I was leaving the room, why did she look at me as if she'd seen a ghost?

Something touched on the edges of her memory but whatever it was, she couldn't bring it to mind.

She shook her head in frustration, and then picked up her violin and began to play.

17

The evening had gone fairly well from Keva's perspective. Matt had walked her across the street to her apartment. She did not ask him up, nor did he seem to expect an invitation. They parted with the understanding that they would get together again when their schedules permitted.

As she made her way up the stairs to her apartment, she stopped for a moment on the landing to listen to music from the floor above. She recognized it as Beethoven's Violin Concerto in D Major.

Where on earth did that come from? I know absolutely nothing about classical music.

****

Keva had deliberately left her cell phone behind for the evening. Upon checking it, she discovered that she'd missed three calls, all of them from her father. He had not left a message.

What could be so important that he would keep calling me?

She entered his number and waited for his hello. "Dad, it's Keva. I see you've been trying to reach me. What's up?"

When he replied, he sounded as if he had been drinking, which was very rare for her father. "I just wanted to hear your voice and tell you I miss you and love you. I'm so sorry for what happened that night, Keva. Your mother and I both are. Do you think you'll ever be able to put it behind you?"

"I'll try, Dad, I'll really try."

They talked for a few more minutes as Keva reassured and comforted her father. He seemed to have been dwelling on the subject of the fire since their last phone call, which was unusual for him. She knew her father was not a man given to introspection.

As Keva ended the call, she realized that she was crying.

We all wanted so much to cling to the myth of the happy family. And now there's no hope of that, we're still grasping desperately for each other's love.

Keva cried herself to sleep that night. She had not felt this alone for a very long time.

Near dawn, she sensed rather than saw the old woman sitting at the end of her bed, as if watching over her.

18

The following week Keva was talking to a young couple, giving them quotes for wedding photographs.

"Do you have a budget for the photography?" she asked the couple.

The young woman bit her lip and looked as if she was about to cry.

Making sure that Arthur was out of earshot, Keva asked, "Do you have friends or family members with a good digital camera who could take photographs at your wedding? Then you could buy a blank album and get prints of your favourite pictures finished off. If you do scrap-booking or know someone who does, you can make up a beautiful photo album at a fraction of the cost."

The young woman looked greatly relieved. "We don't have a lot of money to spend," she conceded.

Keva suggested several places where the couple could buy an inexpensive photo album without the mark-up Arthur charged, and also recommended some online sites that would help the two of them cut down on wedding expenses.

As they left the store, thanking her profusely, she felt a bit guilty for having talked them out of Arthur's professional services.

Oh well. He's got more bookings than he can handle anyway.

She glanced up as the door to the shop opened. It was Matt, and he looked extremely upset. He asked if she could take a walk with him because he needed to talk to her. Keva called to Arthur to let him know that she wanted to go out for a few minutes. She took his garbled reply as an okay.

"What's wrong, Matt?" she asked once they were outside on the sidewalk.

"I heard this morning that the firm isn't doing well. They may have to give pink slips to some of us or close completely. I don't know what I'm going to do. I don't have much in the way of savings. Any extra money I do have, I've put toward my tuition and books for my night courses."

Keva knew that any talk of impending job cuts in this city was always greeted with panic. The federal government had already downsized, and the effects were being felt everywhere: from restaurants and convenience stores to declining ridership for the public transit system. And with ongoing cuts to employment insurance and the rising numbers needing access to food banks, the picture was a bleak one.

"Try to be calm and come up with some alternatives, Matt," she said, thinking how odd it was, given her years of therapy, that she would be counselling someone else.

"Maybe you can cut back on your hours or get financial assistance for your night classes. In the meantime, you should update your résumé. I'm sure that a lot of other firms would welcome someone with your experience. The main thing is to be pro-active."

As she spoke, Keva recognized the irony. *This advice is coming from someone who's spent the last ten years of her life being totally reactive.*

Matt had calmed down a bit. "You're right, of course. It's not really like me to get upset like this, but I've been there long enough to think that I had some job security. I guess that's a thing of the past. Anyway, I better let you get back to work. Thanks for talking to me." He walked her back to the photography studio.

****

Later that evening as she sat at her computer, Keva thought she could again hear music from the floor above.

When she went to sleep that night, she dreamed once more of the dark-haired woman.

When she woke up during the early morning hours, she saw the elderly woman sitting beside her on the bed, stroking her hair.

For once, Keva felt comforted.

For once, she was not afraid.

19

On a warm evening near the end of June, Keva was sitting with her mother in front row seats at Ottawa's National Arts Centre. Myra had been given tickets to an orchestra performance when her friend could no longer attend because of a scheduling conflict. They were both excited because they hadn't been to the NAC for years. The last visit had been when Keva was a child and they had come to see the *Nutcracker Suite*.

Keva still had no idea where her new-found knowledge and appreciation of classical music had originated, but she was recognizing the pieces without the need for a program.

It was time for the violin concerto. Keva's purse had slipped from her lap and as she reached down to retrieve it, she heard the now-familiar strains of Beethoven.

She glanced up to see Ada Schafer playing her violin softly on the stage as the other orchestra members waited for their parts to begin. She wore a long white dress and looked for all the world like an angel.

Perhaps she is my *angel,* Keva mused, not knowing where the thought had come from.

20

"So, Keva, how are you today?" Dr. Finlayson gave her his best approximation of a smile as she entered his office for her counselling session. "Are you sleeping any better?"

She sat in her usual chair, making sure to establish eye contact with him as he settled behind his desk. She had learned after all these years of therapy that eye contact was very important. It showed the therapist that you were getting stronger and asserting control. "I'm still experiencing sleep disturbances, but not as frequently."

"Well, that's a start, anyway."

"I wanted to ask you something, Dr. Finlayson. Is it possible that my, um, condition isn't schizophrenia? I was diagnosed after the fire, but could it have been post-traumatic stress disorder instead? Or a result of depression?"

Dr. Finlayson looked annoyed that she would question a professional diagnosis. After all, he and other therapists had invested a decade in treating her for this mental disorder. "But you responded immediately to the medication we gave you, Keva.

No more voices; no more hallucinations."

That I've told you of.

"Would it be possible for my file to be reviewed? I'm feeling better these days. More assertive. I've been able to reach out to other people." She described how she'd reassured her father on the phone and had given advice to the young couple at her shop and later to her friend Matt.

Dr. Finlayson tried out another one of his ghastly smiles. "I'm very glad to hear this, Keva. But schizophrenia is a condition that requires ongoing medication to regulate it. You can't just abandon your pills."

"No," she reassured him, "I understand that I need the medication if my condition *is* schizophrenia. But I'd really like to be reassessed."

"Well, if you insist on this," he said starchily, "I can have one of my colleagues review your file and talk to you, but—"

She had what she'd come here for. "Thanks so much, Dr. Finlayson. I knew you would understand."

21

Keva had seen Matt several times after their walk that day. The situation at his workplace had been temporarily resolved. The firm's partners had secured a bank loan and had also agreed to take a cut in pay to help keep the company afloat. In turn Matt and the other employees had offered to forgo this year's pay raise. Matt was hopeful that it would all work out.

They were together one evening at his apartment, sitting in the living room and enjoying a movie. It was an unpressured relationship, and they were still at the friendship stage. Keva wasn't certain if she wanted it to go beyond that. But, regardless, she knew it was time for her to confide in him.

As the movie ended, Keva spoke up. "I'd like to talk to you about something, Matt, and I hope you won't be angry that I haven't raised the subject before. It's always been difficult for me to discuss." Her bright green eyes shone with sorrow.

"I'm all ears. Take your time," Matt encouraged her.

"I experienced ... a trauma ... ten years ago. My

parents and I were on vacation in the Thousand Islands. There was a fire in the hotel where we were staying, and I was sent to the hospital because I suffered smoke inhalation. The doctors thought I was displaying symptoms of schizophrenia. I've been in therapy and under medication since that time. I'm feeling much stronger lately—in large part due to our friendship—and I've asked my doctor to review the diagnosis. But I've had a lot of people in my past who couldn't accept my illness."

"I'm glad you told me, Keva, because I sensed that you were holding something back. It won't change anything at all in our relationship. My parents have struggled with depression their whole lives, and they've been very up front about it with me. And I had a close friend who committed suicide because he never got the proper treatment.

"Strange, isn't it, that we don't think twice about someone having a physical illness—other than to wish them a speedy recovery—but it's so different where mental illness is concerned."

"Thank you, Matt," she said very quietly. "Thank you for sticking with me."

22

Keva was feeling much more optimistic after her conversation with Matt. Her mother noticed the change in her demeanour as soon as her daughter arrived at her house for their monthly get-together.

"You're looking much brighter this evening, Keva. Are you feeling better? Getting more sleep?"

"I'm feeling more rested these days and I think I'm coping better. Thanks for noticing, Mom."

"Does this mean you're going to be able to deal with the anniversary?" It was coming up next week.

"I'm going back there, Mom. To the hotel. I need closure. I need to find out . . . what *changed* me there. I can't explain it any other way."

"But what purpose could it possibly serve?It will only set you back just when you're starting to feel better."

"No, I think it will help me. I have a feeling about this, and I need to go through with the return visit. What really happened that night, Mom? How did the fire get started? I think I know how, but I need you to tell me yourself."

Her mother's eyes filled with tears. "I've carried this inside me so long that I guess it's better if I do tell you. You can't hate me any more than I hate myself for what I've done to you."

And then her mother described the events of that night from the familiar tableau constantly playing out in her mind. Afterward she said, "I found you unconscious at the adjoining door. Then the ambulance came for you, and I prayed that you would be okay in spite of what I'd done."

Images of her lying in bed and then getting up to intervene in her parents' argument flashed through Keva's mind. "I remember I was just about to open the connecting door to your room. I had my hand on the knob. I wanted to help you ... to stop the arguing."

Myra wiped the tears from her face. "Poor dear. You always tried so hard to be the peacemaker. But we always kept on arguing, your father and I, didn't we? We were too selfish to think about the toll it was taking on you. How alone you must have felt as the only child."

"It doesn't matter now, Mom, don't you see that? You and Dad and I, we all need to move on with our lives."

"Can you ever forgive me, Keva?"

"Of course, I can, Mom. But you need to forgive yourself."

The Anniversary

23

Although both Matt and her mother had offered to go with her to the hotel in Gananoque, Keva knew it was a trip she needed to make alone. She booked a few days off work, rented a car, and started driving to the hotel. Although she'd kept renewing her driver's licence over the years, she hadn't actually driven a car for some time. This was a good thing, in a way, because it forced her to concentrate on her driving and not on her own thoughts.

When she arrived at the hotel, it seemed much smaller than it had to the seventeen-year-old girl who once stood before it with such excitement. She noticed the signs of wear as she entered the lobby: the carpet was scuffed, there was paint missing where guests had banged their luggage carts against the walls, and there were chips in the granite counter of the front desk.

Strange how this place always stood still in my mind, but in reality it's aged just as I have.

Keva had forgotten the number of the room where they'd stayed a decade ago, but she'd remembered which floor they'd been on. When she signed in, she requested a room on the same floor.

As an afterthought, she asked the desk clerk, "By any chance, were you here during the fire ten years ago?"

"No," he said, shaking his head, "but I've heard other staff speak of it. There was a lot of damage to one floor. Apparently a guest was careless with a cigarette. But I can assure you, miss, that we're a non-smoking hotel now."

"Thanks. I've just got the one bag so I can carry it up. Have a good day."

As she rode the elevator to her room, a sense of déjà vu overwhelmed her. Never one to be claustrophobic, she felt nevertheless that the walls of the elevator were closing in on her. She was relieved when the doors opened on her floor.

The room itself looked vaguely familiar but again there was that strong sense of time having passed: the curtains were frayed, the bedspread looked faded from constant laundering, and the enamel on the compact fridge was scratched.

Now that she was here, Keva had no real idea where to start.

I want closure, but how do I get that? How do I move on?

She was tired after the drive and decided to take a quick nap before doing anything else.

****

Keva awoke with a start and, for a few seconds, couldn't remember where she was. Then she got up and moved around the room, trying to shake off her drowsiness. She noticed the hotel had provided a complimentary copy of a newspaper folded neatly on the corner desk. Keva picked it up, staring absently at it. It was a local paper: the kind that provided human interest stories and was filled with advertisements for small businesses. She flipped through the pages until one article caught her immediate attention:

> *This weekend marks the tenth anniversary of a hotel fire that could easily have turned tragic if Raymond Keller had not been on the job. Keller was one of the paramedics...*

There was a photo of a middle-aged man standing next to an ambulance. The caption read:

> *Raymond Keller: serving our community for over twenty years.*

So many times in my mind I've seen a younger version of that face staring down at me...

Keva grabbed the phone book from the bedside table and turned to the K section to find his number. Her palms were sweaty as she picked up the receiver of the phone and then quickly replaced it.

He's probably at work and anyway what

would I say to him?

She went to the bathroom and splashed her face with cold water, giving herself time to calm down. It took another five minutes for her to compose a conversation in her head.

She decided to use the desk phone in her room rather than her cell phone. The phone rang through and a female voice said hello.

"Yes, could I please speak to Raymond Keller?"

"I'm sorry, he's at work right now. Could I take a message?"

Keva laughed nervously. "This will sound strange but I saw his photo in the paper. I'm staying at the hotel where the fire occurred ten years ago. I was one of the people he helped. I just wanted to say thank you to him."

"Well, I'm sure he'd be very happy to talk to you. His shift ends at eight o'clock this evening. How about I have him call you at the hotel?"

"Thanks so much. Oh, I forgot to give you my name. It's Keva Tait." Keva gave her the phone number and extension.

Now I just have to wait.

She managed to put in the time by taking a walk. It was hot, but the breeze from the water felt wonderful on her skin. She watched the birds circling gracefully overhead. Another feeling of déjà vu. Then she returned to the hotel and ordered room service for a late supper. She wasn't really hungry but thought it would make her feel better to have eaten.

When the phone finally rang, she grabbed it on the first ring and said hello.

"Is this Keva Tait speaking? It's Raymond Keller here. My wife said you'd like to speak to me."

"Thank you so much for calling, Mr. Keller. Your wife probably explained who I am and why I called."

"Yes, she did. My curiosity's got the better of me. Why did you come back to the hotel?"

"I've had a lot of ... problems since that night, not sleeping and, um, other health issues. I thought I could get some closure if I came back here. Probably a silly idea actually."

"No, not at all. It's very common for people who've experienced trauma to want to confront what happened to them and get past it. Kind of like climbing up again on a horse that throws you."

"Thanks. I'm glad you understand. First I wanted to tell you how grateful I am for your help that night. And second, well, I just wanted to know if you remember me." She described herself.

"Yes, of course, the little red-haired lass. Your parents were so frantic. I guess they've talked to you about what happened."

"They've explained that I collapsed from smoke inhalation. And they've reassured me that there were no casualties. The old newspaper articles I've found on the internet confirm this, but I still keep thinking that someone died that night."

There was a pause on the other end of the line. "Did they tell you anything else about your ... condition that night?"

"Only that I was unconscious for awhile. Is there more? Please tell me what you remember from that evening."

"Okay, well, when I brought you out on the stretcher, I checked for a pulse. You didn't have one. I tried giving you CPR for several minutes, but nothing happened. We all thought you were ... gone. I was about to call for the coroner, but then you suddenly started breathing again. If your parents never told you the full story, then you *would* believe that someone had died. You were one lucky young lady."

After Keva finished talking to Raymond Keller, she sat in stunned silence for a few moments. She felt as if she were going backward rather than forward.

What does Ada Schafer have to do with all of this? Why do I keep encountering her and seeing her in my dreams if she wasn't the one who died?

Exhausted, she lay down on the bed and fell asleep on top of the covers.

24

On that long-ago night of the fire, Keva had, in fact, *wanted* to die to escape the burden of her parents. She had seen the drink her mother tried to hide when Keva and her father returned from the play to the hotel room. And later when she hear their loud voices, she knew that the fighting had started all over again.

She might be going away to university, but she would never escape them in her own head. She would always have that almost preternatural sense of foreboding that children living in very unhappy homes often developed. The children who were always waiting for the worst to happen. Always watching their parents closely for signs that the arguments were about to begin. Always terrified that they might end in violence.

Keva felt a little bit of herself dying each time her parents argued, and she blamed herself for their deteriorating relationship. Illogical, of course, but inevitable for a young woman caught between two parents who were self-absorbed and needy.

So on that night ten years ago, she had willed

her body simply *to let go.*

But there had been someone else there, whispering to her. And the voice said:

Don't be afraid, Keva. I mean you no harm.

I am an ancient soul known by many names in my many incarnations.

I sat beside the rivers of Babylon and wept with the others for their exile from Jerusalem.

Throughout the ages, I bore witness to the horrors of war and mankind's inhumanity.

I have seen great suffering. Yet I have also experienced the wonders of compassion and love.

I reside now in the body of another young woman who once lost her way. Several years ago, her parents and siblings suffered violent deaths, and she was burdened with the guilt of the survivor. She tried to join them, but I intervened to help her.

She is from another country, but sorrow is without boundaries.

With my help, she has finally moved on. She has learned simply to rejoice at the small things in life that bring us contentment.

And her music has been a calming influence for her too. I know because I taught her how to play the violin so that she might share her gift with others.

There is still music in this world, Keva, although it's often very hard to hear. Don't give up on your life. Let me help you for a time.

The young Keva had awoken then to the

amazement of the paramedic, Raymond Keller, who thought he had already lost her.

For Keva, the confusion came after the fire because of her inability to accept the ancient soul who co-existed in her body, the guest walk-in who was trying to teach her the way back from the abyss.

Keva had never suffered from schizophrenia. Her struggle had been about choosing the hard alternative of keeping alive.

And the dark-haired woman, both then and now, was Ada Schafer, a symbol of someone who had overcome despair to embrace life. It was Ada's voice, channelled by the ancient soul, that Keva had heard in her head and Ada's spectre she had seen in the mirror and in her dreams long before she met the real Ada Schafer.

****

In the present, the ancient soul, who had manifested itself as an elderly woman to comfort Keva over the past decade, looked down now at her sleeping figure.

Sweet dreams, my love.

It's time for me to move on from you as I did from Ada.

You're ready to stand on your own.

You will remember none of this.

25

Keva awoke on the morning of the anniversary feeling calm and rested. She decided to return home. She had her answers now from Raymond Keller. She had a vague sense that there was more—someone else who had been helping her find her way—but this thought remained on the edge of her consciousness. Perhaps someday she would understand the source in a dream.

She texted her mother and Matt to tell them she was returning home earlier than she'd planned, then checked out of the hotel and began the drive back to Ottawa. She was looking forward to seeing Matt again. He had already proved his loyalty to her. She did not take his friendship lightly.

Once back in Ottawa, she returned the rental car and called a taxi to take her to the apartment. The driver loaded her suitcase in the trunk, and when they were settled in the vehicle, he glanced at her in his rear-view mirror before starting the car. "Did you have a nice trip, miss?"

She smiled at him as she met his eyes in the mirror. "Yes, I did, thank you. But I'm very glad to be home."

Acknowledgments

I would like to thank my husband Mike McCann for suggesting the storyline for "Fire Whisperer"and for reading the draft and providing excellent suggestions for its improvement. It is to Mike and my son Tim that this novella is dedicated.

I knew virtually nothing about schizophrenia when I first started the research for this novella. Since then I've learned that there are twenty-four million people worldwide who are suffering from this illness. Symptoms appear in young adulthood, and the disease occurs more often in males than females. People with schizophrenia are more likely to have major depression and anxiety disorders, as well as substance abuse problems. Long-term unemployment, poverty, and homelessness are common. The life expectancy of a person with schizophrenia is ten- to twenty-five years less than average because of increased physical health problems and a higher suicide rate of five per cent.

Schizophrenia is obviously an illness that requires ongoing funding and research. To learn more, please see http://schizophrenia.com/; http://www.nimh.nih.gov/health/publications/schizophrenia/index.shtml; and http://www.medicinenet.com/schizophrenia/article.htm, http://www.mayoclinic.org/diseases-conditions/schizophrenia/basics/definition/CON-20021077.

For the history of the now-closed Rockwood asylum near Kingston, Ontario, to which Keva alludes, please see http://www.ontariogenealogy. com/kingstoninsaneasylum.html. Women were frequently institutionalized for " 'female trouble— childbirth, lactation, miscarriage, menstrual disorders, uterine disorders' and other natural conditions seen as 'the predisposing cause of insanity.' "

While doing my research for this novella, I came across a poignant story of men and women who were locked away in a New York asylum for most of their lives. In 1995, four hundred suitcases were found in the attic of Willard asylum in upstate New York. A photographer, Jon Crispin, has been documenting these abandoned suitcases, which date from 1910-1960. The average length of stay for patients in this asylum was thirty years. Many patients died there and were buried in graves marked by numbers rather than names. To read this story and to view photographs of the contents of some of the suitcases, please see http://www.dailymail.co.uk/news/ article-2338714/The-chilling-pictures-suitcases- left-New-York-insane-asylum-patients-locked- away-rest-lives.html.

For information on the practice of lobotomy, to which Keva also refers, please see http:// psychology.wikia.com/wiki/Lobotomy and http:// www.livescience.com/42199-lobotomy-definition.

html. The Portuguese neurologist who pioneered this procedure in 1935 won a Nobel Prize for his technique. A lobotomy severed connections in the brain's prefrontal lobe to alter behaviour. This procedure was widely performed for at least two decades to treat schizophrenia, depression, and other mental illnesses prior to the discovery of drugs that could be used for treatment. Some physicians also performed lobotomies on unruly patients who were seen as a disruptive force in their institutions. About 50,000 lobotomies were performed in the United States. The procedure began to be phased out in the 1950s, and was discontinued in the United States by the 1970s, although other countries continued to perform lobotomies during the 1980s.

To read about walk-ins and soul transference/ exchange, please see http://www.crystalinks. com/walk_ins.html; http://healing.about.com/ od/spirituality/a/walk-in-souls.htm; and http:// en.wikipedia.org/wiki/Walk-in. I have used this material as the basis for the online source that Keva queries.

For information on the Ottawa-Carleton Institute of Biology where Gerald Tait obtained his PhD, please see http://www.grad.uottawa. ca/Default.aspx?tabid=1727&page=SubjectDeta ils&Kind=H&SubjectId=24. Under the Ottawa-Carleton Joint Program, graduate students can use the resources and research facilities of both the

University of Ottawa and Carleton University.

The Eagles song to which the younger Gerald Tait refers is "Lyin' Eyes," and the exact quote is "[s]he's so far gone she feels just like a fool."

In response to her daughter wishing her "sweet dreams," the younger Myra Tait admits to herself that she has forgotten how to dream. She is recalling Carly Simon's song "The Way I Always Heard It Should Be": "I hear her call sweet dreams/But I forget how to dream." The elderly soul who resides with Keva wishes her "sweet dreams" before she departs her body, but the phrase is used there in a positive context.

The reference to "the rivers of Babylon" in the ancient soul's speech is from Psalm 137:

> By the rivers of Babylon, there we sat down, yea, we wept, when we remembered Zion./We hanged our harps upon the willows in the midst thereof./For there they that carried us away captive required of us a song; and they that wasted us required of us mirth, saying, Sing us one of the songs of Zion./How shall we sing the LORD's song in a strange land?

Later the ancient soul tells the young Keva that there is still music in the world despite all of mankind's suffering.

When the ancient soul tells Keva that Ada

Schafer has finally learned how to "rejoice," she is recalling Psalm 98:4: "Make a joyful noise unto the LORD, all the earth: make a loud noise, and rejoice..."

There is also an echo of Hagar Shipley in Margaret Laurence's *The Stone Angel*: "I must always, always, have wanted that—simply to rejoice. How is it I never could?"

And the name "Ada" in German means "joy."

Finally, if you're considering a vacation in or want to learn more about the beautiful Thousand Islands area, please see http://1000islands.com/ and http://www.visit1000islands.com/. You can rest assured, by the way, that the account of the hotel fire is a fiction for the sake of the story.

Circle of Souls

In memory of my brothers, Alan, Jimmy, and Johnny, and my sisters, Janet and Joan, who died much too young, but who still live on in my heart.

Part 1

Disturbances

1

Erin Murphy draped her sweater around her shoulders. There was a definite chill in the air. She was upstairs in a small, cramped room in the canal museum that she was using as a research base. It was January and she was taking advantage of the fact that the museum was closed to the general public during this month. A graduate student at Carleton University in Ottawa, Erin was researching the history of the Rideau Canal in preparation for her doctoral thesis and had permission to use the archives at the museum.

It was 9 PM and she was getting sleepy. During the day, she marked papers and tutored students at the university in return for scholarship funding, which meant that most of her research had to be done in the evening.

The museum in which Erin currently sat had a reputation for being haunted. There had been many stories of ghostly activity from both museum staff and visitors. Erin herself was a skeptic as far as the supernatural was concerned, but she had to admit that she always felt vaguely uneasy here.

Unfortunately, the documents she was consulting were too valuable and too fragile to be removed from the museum.

Her cell phone rang and she looked at the caller ID to see who it was, thinking that it was probably her husband checking to see what time she wanted to be picked up. But the caller ID showed "Blocked Call" and when she answered there was only static on the line and then a shrill screech, as if someone had mistakenly dialled her phone number instead of a fax number. She quickly pressed the End button.

The phone started up again shortly, but this time it was her husband calling. "Hi, Seth. Good timing. It's freezing here, and I'm getting really sleepy. You can pick me up any time."

"Be there soon. Love you, Erin."

She started to reply but then realized that he had already ended the call.

The phone rang again almost immediately, and she answered it, thinking that Seth had forgotten to tell her something. But it was the same static she had heard before, although she thought she also heard a faint voice murmuring in the background.

Something about the sound disturbed her, sending a chill down her spine. She ended the call and decided if the phone rang again, she would let it go to voice mail.

Erin gathered her coat and purse and locked away the papers she'd been reviewing in a glass cabinet. Seth always knocked on the downstairs door of the museum when he arrived, saying that he thought it was rude to honk his horn instead. He was thoughtful like that.

As she started down the stairs, holding the railing out of reflex because they were narrow and poorly lit, she was lost in thought, still wondering if she had actually heard a background voice in the last call.

She sensed movement behind her. Suddenly she felt a strong hand pushing her in the small of her back. She lurched forward but had a tight enough grip on the railing to avoid a fall.

She looked back, but there was no one there.

Unnerved, she hurried down the stairs to the front door, opening it just as her husband was about to knock, and heaved a huge sigh of relief at the sight of him.

On the drive home, Erin debated whether to tell Seth about the incident on the stairs, but was reluctant to do so. After all, it made no sense to her, and she simply wasn't ready to accept a "ghostly" explanation. She chalked it up to being tired and preoccupied. She had probably just stumbled.

She had not glimpsed the shadowy figure watching her from the top of the stairs.

2

Seth Thomas was a tall, gangly, bearded man with thick glasses. He always made jokes about his nerdy appearance, but in fact he had that "little boy lost" air about him that females were often drawn to. It was his kindness and sense of humour that first attracted Erin to him. They had been married for a little over a year now, having met as undergraduates at the university. They lived in an apartment building on McLaren Street, one of the newer ones that had underground parking.

Seth was a lecturer in English at the university, for which he received a modest income. He was completing his thesis in his spare time and hoped eventually to obtain a tenure-track position. They were able to pay their rent and buy groceries with their combined income, with very little left over for savings or entertainment.

The car was an extravagance for them: they had discussed whether it was better to sell it and use the bus to get around the city like most other graduate students did. It was an old Chevy Malibu that had several recall notices on it, but it still managed to function, and they had decided to keep it, enjoying the convenience and freedom it provided. When they were particularly overwhelmed by the traffic and construction in the city, they would take a trip to a country farmers' market or window shop in the artist boutiques in nearby Merrickville.

While Seth had grown up in the city, Erin had been raised in the small village of Burritts Rapids. Her mother was a descendant of Stephen Burritt, whose family first settled the area and for whom the town was named, and she was active in the local historical society. Erin grew up learning the history of the area and always wanting to know more. A major in history was a natural for her.

Once the car was parked and locked, Erin and Seth took the elevator up to their apartment. It was a one-bedroom which they had decorated with finds from flea markets and yard sales. The kitchen was too small for a table so they ate on TV trays in the living room, which also doubled as a study. There was a corner desk which they both shared.

"How'd it go tonight, Erin?" Seth asked as they ate their Michelina dinners and a Caesar salad with wilted lettuce that Seth had prepared. He was a quiet man and a good listener. He always acted as Erin's sounding board.

"Good. I'm doing more research on the Irish immigrants who worked on the canal and later in the lumber trade. There are a lot of documents at the museum that I still need to read, but I've got the place to myself for the rest of the month so I decided to pack it in early tonight. I'm bushed. How did your day go, Seth? You had to give a lecture on William Blake, didn't you?"

Seth laughed ruefully. "It's so difficult to connect with these kids. I feel more like their babysitter than their instructor. All they want to know is whether they're going to be tested on the material and whether they should take notes. They spend most of their time texting and don't listen to me anyway. But I explained to them how Blake had created his own mythology and showed them reproductions of some of his engravings, and it seemed to resonant with them as if Blake were a forefather of today's graphic novelists. Whatever it takes, I guess, to keep them interested."

They cleaned up from supper, shared some ice cream for dessert, and watched the local news before going to bed.

But Erin was restless, and her sleep was troubled.

Shortly after midnight, she startled awake.

In her nightmare, she had been about to step off a precipice and plunge into the darkness below.

3

Lloyd Sumner was a videographer who worked as a freelancer. He was a young man in his late twenties, bearded, and of average build. At the moment, he was standing outside the main entrance to the canal museum waiting for Muriel Spears, the curator, to arrive to unlock the door. He had been commissioned by the City of Ottawa to do a video of the museum that would be used on its website. Lloyd was vaguely aware that the museum was one of the places that was visited on Ottawa's haunted tours, but he had been advised that the video should focus on the historical exhibits to encourage cultural tourism.

"Sorry I'm running late," Muriel said as she hurried to shake Lloyd's hand. "My car wouldn't start. Had to get a boost."

"No problem. I just got here myself."

"Have you visited our museum before?"

"A long time ago on a school outing."

Muriel laughed as she opened the door and ushered him inside. "School children seem to fixate on certain displays, especially the plaster cast of

Thomas D'Arcy McGee's hand. Do you know the story behind that, by the way?" She took his coat and hung it up in a small cloakroom off the entrance way.

"I know that he was a Father of Confederation who was assassinated on Sparks Street. I'm afraid I don't know much more than that."

Muriel led him to the cast of the hand, which looked macabre to Lloyd, as if a body had been dismembered. He shuddered involuntarily, but tried to make light of it. "It's a bit like Thing in *The Addams Family*, isn't it?"

Frowning slightly and not seeming to understand Lloyd's reference, Muriel continued her explanation. "Thomas D'Arcy McGee was killed in 1868 and at that time it was customary to make a plaster 'death mask' of the deceased. Because of the damage done by the bullet, however, they made a cast of his writing hand instead, which was fitting because he was a gifted writer and orator."

Muriel continued her narrative of the provenance of various items in the museum, taking him on a tour of each floor. She left the basement, which contained the original stone vault, to the end.

"This building was originally a Commissariat constructed to store supplies and wages for the Rideau Canal workers and to serve as a military base, if need be. The canal was designed to provide an alternate route to Kingston because the Americans had blocked off the St. Lawrence passage from Montreal during the War of 1812.

"The Commissariat was under the control of General Duncan McNab, and he did a good job of guarding it, let me tell you. There were no break-ins at all under his watch.

"You've probably heard some of the ghost stories about this museum. Some people speculate that it's the ghost of Duncan McNab haunting this place, but I don't think so. General McNab had a sense of humour from all accounts, and the ghost or ghosts haunting this place can be quite malicious, I'm told. I've never experienced anything myself," she hastened to add.

Lloyd started the videotaping with the vault and worked his way up to the third floor, pausing to film the various major exhibits and the archives. A voice-over narrative would be added once they decided what footage to use.

"We have a graduate student from Carleton University doing archival research right now," Muriel explained. "Of course, we don't have nearly as many reference works as the National Archives, but there is a lot of interesting material here on the canal and its builders."

Lloyd had finished the taping, and as he gathered his equipment and retrieved his coat, he thanked the curator for the tour and for the information she'd provided. He thought that with her bountiful knowledge and strong, clear voice she would be the perfect candidate to do the voice-over. He would mention it to his contact at the City of Ottawa.

4

Jim Evans, the head of a local paranormal society, began setting up video equipment and audio recorders, as well as handing out pads and pencils to the members of his team. He was a short, stocky man in his late thirties whose earnestness instilled trust in his clients.

Although paranormal research is still considered a pseudo-science, Jim and his group members tried to be as meticulous as possible in their investigations. They were accustomed to ridicule from both the "evangelical" believers in the paranormal and the skeptics, but they were trained in their craft and viewed themselves as professionals.

They were here by invitation investigating an old mill in Manotick, a small town outside Ottawa. The mill had a tragic history and was believed to be haunted. In the nineteenth century, the mill belonged to a rich owner who spared no expense in outfitting it with the latest equipment. When the owner brought his young bride to the mill to show it off to her, the skirt of her hooped dress caught in the shafts of one of the machines and she was thrown against a support beam. She died instantly, and her husband sold his share of the mill to his partner and abandoned the site forever.

Jim and his group were on the second floor of the mill where the accident had occurred. It was almost noon. Contrary to popular belief, paranormal activity can occur at any time of the day, not only under the cover of darkness. It was around 1 PM--the hour at which the mill-owner's wife died--that most of the paranormal episodes were said to occur. There were reports both of the sounds of a female weeping and the sighting of a woman at a second-floor window. Jim thought that both could be examples of pareidolia—seeing images such as a human face in a random pattern of light and hearing sounds where there were none.

Once the equipment was set up, he and his team sat back to wait. It is another popular misconception that such investigations automatically result in findings. In fact, some sites have been investigated for years without yielding results to paranormal investigators.

Fortunately, Jim was a patient man.

5

Erin woke up early that morning after having experienced a restless night. She decided to spend a few hours at the museum before her tutoring appointments began in the afternoon.

Seth was already up and making coffee because he had to prepare for his morning lecture. She joined him in the kitchen, standing on her tiptoes to give him a good morning kiss. There was about a six-inch difference in their height. Erin envied the fact that her husband could eat anything and stay so skinny. She herself had a fondness for sweets and was a bit chubby—a word she secretly hated, preferring to think of herself as having a well-rounded figure.

She poured a cup of coffee and opened the living room curtains to catch a few minutes of winter sunshine.

"Do you mind leaving a bit early for your class and dropping me off at the museum?"

"Sure thing. Does that mean you won't have to go there tonight, and we can spend an evening together? Maybe even order in a pizza?"

"Sounds great to me. That place is really creepy at night, by the way. And cold."

"I don't doubt it. Doesn't Martha say it's got bad karma?"

Martha was a close friend who read eclectically and enjoyed books on the supernatural. She had accompanied Erin once to the museum and pronounced-- as soon as she entered the building-- that it had bad vibes.

"I think she's right," Erin said, and Seth was surprised by the seriousness of her tone.

He dropped her off at the museum and, as Erin unlocked the door and entered the building, she was surprised to hear voices inside.

Muriel Spears came over to her with a young man in tow. "Hi, Erin. This is Lloyd, who's videotaping the museum for the upcoming tourist season. I'm afraid I've been bending his ear. Lloyd, this is Erin, the graduate student I told you about who's using our archives for research."

As Erin and Lloyd shook hands, Erin apologized to Muriel for disturbing them.

"No problem, Erin. Lloyd won't be filming the offices upstairs."

"I'll leave you to it, then. Nice to meet you, Lloyd," Erin said as she headed up the stairs to the fourth floor.

As she entered the small office that doubled as her research area for books and papers that were sturdy enough to be moved from the archives on the lower floor, Erin felt the same chill she had experienced last evening. She adjusted her sweater and returned to the documents she'd been examining. They contained a description and rough, hand-drawn map of Corktown, where the Irish labourers from County Cork in Ireland had lived while building the Rideau Canal.

Construction of the canal began in 1826 under the direction of Colonel John By—in fact, Ottawa was known as Bytown at that time—and the shanties that comprised Corktown spread from Somerset Road to the current site of Ottawa's National Arts Centre. It was amusing, Erin thought, that staid Ottawa was once a rowdy place with brothels and taverns throughout Corktown. The name still resonated in the area: the Somerset footbridge that connected the University of Ottawa to Centretown was commonly referred to as the Corktown bridge.

But the papers also told of the poverty of the workers and the spread of malaria among them and their families. In fact, it was estimated that one thousand workers died during the construction of the canal, and most of their deaths were attributable to malaria.

Erin knew that many of the workers and their families had been buried on grounds close to the canal. When excavations were being made for the new light rail transit system in Ottawa in 2013, one of the burial sites had been disturbed. Because the graves had been marked with wooden crosses, which had since rotted with age, many of the skeletal remains could not be identified. She recalled reading that provincial authorities had posted notices in newspapers in an effort to locate any relatives you wished to claim the remains before they were moved to cemeteries for proper burial.

Erin decided to take a break from her reading. She went to the small kitchen nearby and made a pot of coffee. She was pouring herself a cup when she heard voices below. Thinking it was Muriel Spears and the videographer, she descended the stairs to investigate.

There was no one there.

Puzzled, she returned to the kitchen to discover that her cup had been emptied, washed, and stacked on the dish rack to dry.

I'm the only one here, and I only left for a few seconds. What's going on?

Clearly unnerved by the incident, Erin decided to forgo the coffee and return to her work. She spend several more hours doing research on the demographics of Bytown, both before and after the building of the canal.

She made some notes on her yellow legal pad and then decided to call it a day. She would transfer the information to her laptop tomorrow. She preferred to make long-hand notes because they focused her attention, and when she transcribed them to her computer, she had a second opportunity to verify dates and ensure the accuracy of the information.

Erin decided to catch a bus to the university for her afternoon tutoring appointments, and then catch up with Seth after his classes.

As she gathered up her belongings, her cell phone rang in her hand. She pressed the Talk button without checking caller ID and was immediately relieved that it was Seth at the other end, calling to see how she was doing.

This place is really starting to get to me. What did I expect to hear—a voice from the grave?

6

Erin was glad to be at home for an evening with her husband. They were both so busy lately that they'd had almost no time together. They ordered a pizza and watched an old science fiction movie on television.

"Everything okay, Erin? You seem a bit distracted these days. Is the research going okay?"

"Yes, it's going fine. I think I'm just a bit overtired. I haven't been sleeping that well."

"Maybe once your research is finished at the museum, we can use our mad money to take a short trip. How's that sound to you?"

"Sounds good. Once I finish at the museum, I have some additional work to do at the National Archives. Maybe we can go after that if your schedule's clear."

"It's a deal. Let's go to bed and we can clean the kitchen up in the morning. I'll help you relax," he replied, winking at her.

Seth woke up around 2 AM and saw that Erin was struggling in her sleep, as if in the throes of a nightmare. He gently shook her shoulder, and she settled into a more peaceful sleep. He lay awake for an hour, stroking her hair and thinking how terrible it would be to lose her.

Where on earth did that thought come from? he wondered.

In her nightmare Erin was staring at a disintegrated face that seemed to float in the air and leer at her. She was back in the museum. It was night. She heard someone quietly weeping, but could see no one.

Suddenly the walls also started weeping. The face that leered at her opened its blackened mouth and screamed, "GET OUT!"

Then she felt a gentle touch on her shoulder, and everything seemed to be all right again.

When the alarm sounded at 7 AM, Erin looked for Seth beside her as she silenced the clock radio. He wasn't there. She heard him moving around in the kitchen and could smell the coffee brewing. She sat up and grabbed her robe.

In her mind Erin saw the fleeting image of a leering face. She shuddered.

"Morning, darling. I thought I'd get up a bit early and make us breakfast. As you can see, I forgot to turn the alarm off. I planned to let you sleep in a bit."

"That's okay. I needed to get up anyway."

Seth watched his wife affectionately as she poured herself a cup of coffee. With her hair tousled and her eyes still full of sleep, she looked like a ten year old. Then he noticed the fatigue lines around her eyes.

"Not enough sleep again?" he asked.

"No, too many bad dreams. It'll probably sound silly to you, but that old museum is starting to get to me. I think I should call Ghostbusters." Erin tried to make light of the subject, but her grim expression belied her attempt at humour.

7

Lloyd Sumner finished the last of his breakfast, poured a second cup of coffee, and then began to watch the video footage of the canal museum on his computer. He was pleased with it. The images were clear, and he had been able to highlight the plaster hand of Thomas D'Arcy McGee, the bust of Colonel By, and the maps and photographs in the glass-enclosed exhibits that told an intriguing story of the history of the Rideau Canal and the lumber trade that helped to build Canada.

Lloyd especially liked the footage of the stone vault that he had juxtaposed with old photographs of casks of liquor that at one time had been stored there.

He went to refill his coffee. When he returned and resumed his review of the video footage, he saw the display of antique dolls that he had filmed. He was mesmerized by the detailed features of the dolls and how well they had been preserved.

Suddenly, one of the dolls moved, and her eyes stared straight at him.

Startled, he replayed the footage of the dolls several times. But they just sat there primly, staring vacantly from the screen.

8

The canal museum where Erin was currently doing her research is not the only one in Ottawa reputed to be haunted. The much larger nature museum, a massive stone structure commonly known as "the castle," has its own history of hauntings. The museum had at one time been used as a headquarters for the Canadian Parliament after fire damaged the Parliament Buildings. The body of one of Canada's prime ministers, Sir Wilfrid Laurier, once lay in state at the museum.

Cathy Davis had recently accepted a job at the nature museum and was currently working on a fossil that had been damaged in transit to the facility. She had undergraduate degrees in biology and anthropology, as well as training in museology and fossil conservation, and had spent many summers in field digs in the Alberta Badlands. She'd loved dinosaurs since she was a small child playing with her set of plastic reptiles, and a school visit to this very museum to view the dinosaur exhibits had strengthened her resolve to make this her life's work. At the age of thirty-two she felt herself privileged to be working here. It had been a long haul juggling several part-time jobs to keep herself afloat until she'd finally been able to find an opening. Restoration was a very specialized field— one in which she excelled because of her patience, knowledge, and dedication.

Of course, she had heard the various stories of eerie sounds, doors opening and closing on their own, electrical equipment coming unplugged by itself, and elevators moving from floor to floor with no one inside. She herself had felt the various "cold spots"in the museum, but thought they could be attributed to drafts. It was, after all, a very old building. She was more concerned about the fact that her tools were constantly disappearing and reappearing in the wrong place without any logical explanation.

The museum was about to close for the day, and Ben Jones, the head of security and a veteran of twenty years at the museum, was making the rounds with a new security guard in tow, showing him how to do a sweep to ensure no visitor was left behind after closing hours. There was a large turnover of security guards at the nature museum, which was rumoured to be linked to its haunted status. Cathy thought it probably had more to do with the nature of the occupation: security guards were always looking for higher paying jobs just like everyone else in the service industry.

"Hello, Ms. Davis. Are you working late tonight?" Ben asked, as he introduced the new guard to her.

"Probably for a couple more hours. I'll make sure I lock up after me when I leave."

"We've had some trouble with kids trying to stay after hours. Those Ben Stiller movies might have made museums more popular, but there's always a school kid or two now who dares another one to spend the night here."

Cathy laughed. "I think they'd find it quite boring. I haven't seen any dinosaurs come to life lately."

Cathy knew she was spending more and more of her time at the museum, but she was still trying to recover from her divorce from Jack Davis the previous year. She felt so alone when she returned to her apartment at the end of the day. Aside from an occasional visit with her brother Seth and his wife Erin, she didn't have much of a social life.

I owe Seth and Erin a meal because they cooked the last one. Maybe this weekend, if Erin's not too busy with her research.

After a few hours of painstaking work to restore the fossil, she was getting tired and decided to call it a day. She straightened up her work area, replaced her tools, and carefully locked the fossil away.

As she was about to leave her workstation and get her coat, Cathy felt a sudden tap on her shoulder. Thinking it was a security guard, she turned around expectantly to tell him she was just leaving. But no one was there.

9

If there's a "most haunted" among Ottawa's haunted sites, this honour would probably go to the former jail, now a youth hostel. Another old and massive stone building like the nature museum, the jail had seen more than its share of human misery until it was finally closed in 1972. The hanging rope that officially ended the lives of those sentenced to death before Canada abolished capital punishment is still displayed at the jail. There are also stories of unofficial hangings of "troublesome" prisoners from the main stairway of the prison.

Patrick Whelan, found guilty of the murder of Thomas D'Arcy McGee in 1868 and hanged in the jail the following year, was its most famous prisoner. There are still many who dispute his guilt and maintain that he was railroaded by the police and the courts, who were looking for a quick end to a highly publicized case. The haunting of the jail is often attributed to the ghost of this man, still seeking justice.

Of course, this made for an interesting story

on Ottawa's haunted tours, but Sarah Bennett, who worked as a tour guide, thought that there were many other likely candidates for ghosthood given the despair the jail had engendered. She could not imagine why anyone would want to stay in this place—even for one night—and was always relieved when this part of the haunted tour ended. It was a part-time job for her. The busiest time was in October in the lead-up to Halloween, but the public could also schedule tours between November and April.

Sarah was doing an undergraduate degree in English at Carleton University, and the money from her job went toward her tuition fees. Once, during a lecture on the Gothic tradition in English romantic literature, she had pointed out to her instructor, Seth Thomas, that fascination with the supernatural was now fuelling a billion dollar "ghost" adventure industry.

Sarah was uncomfortable admitting to herself that the unexplained noises she heard, the displacement of objects from one tour to the next, and the clanging shut of cell doors with no one present defied rational explanation.

10

Erin decided to take a break from the canal museum to consolidate her notes and determine which documents she still needed to review. Seth was busy at the university so she figured she would do some housecleaning and cooking ahead to freeze for meals. *Man—or woman—cannot live by pizza and Michelina dinners alone*, she thought. The idea of staying at home for the day cheered her up. She had felt so depressed lately.

Her cell phone rang around 9 AM as she was getting a wash ready. It was Seth's sister Cathy.

"Hi, Erin. Hope I didn't get you at a bad time. Do you have a minute to talk?"

"I'd love to. I'm at home today so it's a good time for us to catch up on gossip."

"Great. I called to invite you and Seth to my place on Saturday. It's my turn to cook a meal. I thought we could eat around seven. Are you guys free?"

"Yes, we'd really enjoy that. Seth's been busy with lectures and grading papers, and I've been doing a ton of research. It will give us something to look forward to.

"How's everything going with your job, by the way? Are you still enjoying it?"

There was a slight hesitation in Cathy's voice as she answered. "It's going well, if you don't count the weird stuff that happens around there."

"What weird stuff, Cathy?" Erin asked, suddenly concerned.

"I think I'm letting the stories about the place being haunted get to me. I was working late last night, and I'm sure I felt someone tap me on the shoulder, but there was no one there."

"Are you having trouble sleeping as well?" Erin interrupted.

"Yes ... I am. How did you know?"

"Believe it or not, I'm experiencing some weird stuff at *my* museum too. Actually, that's why I'm home today. I couldn't face another day there right now. And I haven't been sleeping well. I wake up exhausted."

They talked for several minutes, comparing notes on their experiences. Then Cathy had to end the conversation to get ready for work, but she assured Erin that they would talk more on Saturday.

Erin decided to give Martha a call before she went back to her housework. The pretext was that she hadn't spoken to her friend for awhile, but Erin knew the real reason was to discuss the canal museum with her.

Martha was one of a kind: in addition to her

full-time course load at the university, she served as a volunteer at the Salvation Army and the animal shelter. She was also a member of Amnesty International and a campaigner for prisoners' rights. Martha had an open and inquiring mind, and currently she was delving into New Age and fringe philosophies.

Martha answered on the first ring. "Martha speaking, but not the vineyard." She had a fondness for changing her greeting for each call she received.

"Hi, Martha not the vineyard. It's Erin. We haven't talked for a while and I'm taking the day off to putter around the apartment. How're you doing?"

"Oh, hi, Erin. I was just thinking of you. Do-doo, Do-doo—*Twilight Zone*, eh! I'm up to my eyeballs in essays and seminars, but what else is new. How are *you* doing? I haven't seen you since that time I visited your creepy museum."

This was the opening Erin wanted. She confided in Martha about the incidents at the museum—the push in the back, the displacement of the coffee cup, and the voices she heard there, before telling her about her nightmares.

"Okay, I think we need to rally the troops here. I have a friend who can help us. She's a psychic— sorry, I mean a *sensitive*. That's the term she prefers. She's done stuff with paranormal investigators. I can give her a call—"

"Hold off for now, Martha," Erin interrupted, "but thanks for the offer. I just needed to talk this out with someone who wouldn't laugh at me. I'll keep in touch with you and let you know if I need an intervention. Thanks again for listening."

After promising Martha that she would be careful and would keep her posted, Erin ended the phone call. She felt better having Martha on her side.

11

Seth Thomas looked up from the papers he was grading in his small office at the university when he heard a knock at the door.

"Come in, please. Oh hi, it's Sarah, isn't it? Have a seat. How can I help you?" He recognized the tall, bespectacled young woman who seemed so serious in his class and always sat in one of the front rows, taking copious long-hand notes.

"Hi, Professor Thomas. I have a favour to ask. I know that we're doing *The Picture of Dorian Gray* this term, but I was wondering if for my next essay, I could do it on *The Ballad of Redding Gaol.*" She then explained what her part-time job was. "After seeing the cells at the old jail, I think I can really understand how Oscar Wilde felt when he wrote that poem."

"I think that would be an excellent choice. And if you're interested, the class would probably enjoy a talk from you on the history of the jail. Many of your classmates aren't from Ottawa, and even the ones who are may not know much about Ottawa's history. My wife's doing her PhD in history. She's conducting research right now at the canal museum."

"That's interesting. That's one of our stops on the haunted tour. It's amazing how many places in Ottawa are rumoured to be haunted. There's the canal museum and the nature museum; the former jail; the Grant House, where Dr. Grant supposedly had a morgue in his basement; the old Lisgar Collegiate School whose top floor's been converted to storage because everyone's afraid to go up there; and of course the Fairmont Chateau Laurier. Do you know the story behind that, by the way?"

Seth smiled. "No, I've never heard it."

"The builder of the hotel was en route to its grand opening. Unfortunately, he was sailing on the *Titanic*. He was one of its many casualties. The story is that his ghost still lives in the hotel. Of course, there are other stories too, but this is usually the one you hear most often.

"Anyway, thank you for letting me choose that poem for my essay. Speaking of which, I should let you get back to your marking," Sarah said, trying not to be too obvious as she looked to see whose paper he was grading.

"I'll look forward to reading your essay, Sarah."

As he returned to his marking, Seth smiled. He found it amusing that a city as conservative as

Ottawa had so many haunted house stories to offer. He wondered if anyone actually believed them.

12

Seth returned home that evening to a pristine apartment and a home-cooked meal. He was pleased to see Erin looking so happy.

"You look wonderful. Did you spend the day at the spa or was it your secret lover who put that smile on your face? I thought I saw someone climbing out of our bedroom window as I was parking the car," Seth teased. They were on the eighteenth floor of the apartment building.

"Silly fool," she said fondly as she stood on tiptoes to give him a kiss. "I took a break today. Did some housework because our books were taking over the apartment," she said, referring to the research books and novels that they both left open wherever they happened to be sitting. "I did some cooking too, and froze some stuff ahead. Speaking of food, Cathy called and invited us over Saturday for supper."

"Good. We need the break, and Cathy sure needs the company. She's become almost a recluse since her divorce. Maybe we can splurge on some wine and flowers to bring her."

He put away his coat and started helping Erin set up the TV trays for supper. "Wow, this looks good, and the place looks great. Where'd you hide all our junk?"

"I'm not admitting to anything, but just be careful when you open the hall closet."

After supper, Erin decided it was time to broach the subject of the incidents at the canal museum. Seth looked concerned as she described how someone had tried to push her down the stairs. "But how could that happen? You were the only one in the museum."

"I honestly don't know and at the time I tried to convince myself that I'd imagined it, but now I'm sure I didn't. And I tried to tell myself that the voices I heard were just the walls settling and the coffee incident was a matter of forgetting that I'd finished my coffee and was cleaning up. But that just doesn't wash with me, pardon the pun. I think these incidents are real. You know me, Seth. If anything, I'd probably be accused of being too literal as opposed to overimaginative."

Seth looked perplexed. "There must be a rational explanation. I just can't think of one right now."

13

On Saturday evening, Seth and Erin headed for Cathy's apartment. Erin had forewarned him that his sister was experiencing similar unexplained incidents at the nature museum. He was thus prepared for some unusual conversation that evening.

Cathy, who was tall and reed-thin like her brother, greeted them at the door. Seth was surprised to see how tired and drawn her face looked, as if a recent illness had sapped her strength.

"How've you been, sis? Did you get hit with that flu bug that's making the rounds?" he asked as he hugged her.

"No. I get the flu shot every year. I think it's just the January blahs," she said, not very convincingly. "Come on in. Supper's almost ready. I've got your favourite: grilled salmon and roasted veggies."

After they'd finished eating, Erin helped her sister-in-law load the dishwasher and make coffee. "Great meal, Cathy. Thanks so much for having us over. I've filled Seth in on what's been happening so he's prepared for our conversation."

Cathy filled the coffee cups and placed them on a tray, which she carried into the living room. "So, kid brother, I hear Erin's been telling you about all the strange goings-on at our respective museums."

"Yeah, what's up at your workplace, Cathy? Are you still having 'incidents', for lack of a better word?" Seth asked.

"Actually, I've had a few more weird experiences since I spoke to Erin. This time with the elevators. I call one up, and the button's always pressed for another floor even though the elevator's empty. A couple of times I've gone to the other floor to see if anyone's summoning it, and there's never anyone there. Of course, someone could have decided to get off the elevator before his stop, but I find it hard to believe that this would happen so often. Especially at night when there are so few of us working. And the number of times that the elevator stops near my workstation and is empty is just downright creepy."

"Erin said you haven't been sleeping well," Seth interjected.

"You know, Seth, that I'm one of the soundest sleepers in the world. Remember when we were still at home how Mom had to call me several times before I got up for school?"

"I do indeed." Seth smiled at the memory of his sister arriving late for almost every breakfast.

"Well, now I fall asleep and I feel like there's

literally someone sitting on my chest. I wake up, and it takes me an hour or so to get back to sleep. Then it happens all over again. I know I've been celibate since my divorce, but I don't think I need an incubus," she joked feebly.

Seth shook his head, not knowing what to say. "Maybe you should see a doctor, sis, and rule out a physical cause." In truth, he was more concerned about her *mental* health. Could her solitude following the divorce have triggered any of this?

14

Erin spent the next week working evenings at the canal museum. To her relief, nothing strange happened. She was close to finishing her research and was looking forward to the day she no longer had to come back here. She'd already noted a direct correlation between time spent at the museum and her nightmares.

As she arrived at the museum late that Thursday afternoon, she heard the curator call out to her.

"Hi, Erin. You remember Lloyd, who's doing the filming here. He's edited the film and brought it back to see what I think of it. Why don't you sit with us? Always good to have another pair of eyes. Let me know what you think." She ushered Erin into a closet-size room that they were using as the viewing area.

Erin exchanged pleasantries with Lloyd, and then located an extra chair . She watched the screen as the various exhibits were highlighted and nodded approvingly as the vault appeared on screen with a close-up of its marvellous stone masonry.

She noticed that Lloyd stiffened slightly at one point in the film and wondered why. It was simply a display of the lovely antique dolls that formed part of one exhibit. "Those dolls are amazingly life-like," she started to comment, but then froze mid-sentence as the doll in the far-right corner of the screen began to cry.

Erin gasped, and the curator turned to her. "Everything, okay, Erin? You look like you've seen a ghost."

"I, um, thought I saw something on the screen. Just my imagination, I guess." But then she noticed that Lloyd was looking down at the table and would not meet her eyes, as if he too

had seen something, but did not wish to acknowledge it.

The viewing was finally over, and Erin complimented him on his work, leaving the room quickly to go upstairs. She sat down in the desk chair in her office and tried to collect her thoughts.

She *knew* what she had seen. The doll had been staring vacantly ahead, like the other ones in the frame, when suddenly its eyes had brimmed with moisture. A single tear had rolled down the doll's face.

Erin shook her head, as if to dismiss these thoughts as lunacy. She removed the papers she'd been reviewing from their glass case and tried to concentrate on them. It seemed to work and within a few minutes she was absorbed in the history of the local timber barons.

Bytown had been a major hub for sawmills and the distribution of lumber, which was rafted down the Ottawa River for eventual sale to Britain and later to the United States when the Reciprocity Treaty took effect to allow free trade between the two countries. The documents were an intriguing mix of newspaper clippings, hand-drawn diagrams of the slides, cribs, and rafts used to move the lumber, and old bills of lading. It was fascinating to see first-hand documents relating to the people who helped build the city: the lumber barons Philemon Wright, who was the founder of Hull, Quebec; Henry Franklin Bronson; and J.R. Booth, whose sawmill had supplied lumber for the construction of Canada's Parliament Buildings.

The inter-connectivity of names was also fascinating: Nicholas Sparks, for whom Sparks Street in Ottawa is named, was an employee of the lumber baron Philemon Wright, whose son Ruggles had built the first timber slide on the Ottawa River that allowed loggers to bypass the nearby Chaudière Falls. The navigation of the falls before the invention of the slide, Erin read, was very dangerous and resulted in many fatalities.

One of the documents in particular caught her attention: it was a bill of lading for lumber provided for the building of a house commissioned by Joseph Merrill Currier. *Why does that name sound so familiar?* Erin wondered. Then she remembered that he'd been the owner of the old mill in nearby Manotick and had fled to Ottawa and never returned to the town after his young bride died violently at the mill. In fact, she had read somewhere that many people thought his wife's ghost was still haunting the mill. Currier had subsequently married the daughter of Ruggles Wright and settled into this grand house, which was now the home to Canada's Prime Minister at 24 Sussex Drive.

Erin looked at her watch and realized she'd been studying these documents for almost three hours. She stood, stretching, and then began tidying up the desk. Seth had texted her that he'd be coming soon to pick her up.

She grabbed her coat and headed down the stairs. On her way out, she happened to glance at the doll exhibit. Nothing seemed out of place, but when she looked closer she saw that the doll she'd seen crying in Lloyd's videotape was bent over. As she reached down to straighten it, she discovered the doll's dress and face were wet, as though with the remnants of tears.

A sudden knock at the door startled her, and she cried out.

"Erin, what's wrong? Open the door now," Seth called from the outside. He sounded panicked.

"I'm okay. You just startled me is all," Erin said, as she flung the door open.

"Why are you crying, Erin? What's happened?" He pulled her close to him.

"Don't be silly, I'm not crying." But then he touched her face, and Erin saw that his hand came away wet.

"Let's go, now," she said. "Let's get out of here. We can talk at home."

Erin locked the museum door, and started to walk toward the car. "Did you leave the high beams on by accident, Seth?"

"What the hell," Seth exclaimed as he looked at the vehicle.

Not only were the high beams on, sweeping the darkness, but the wipers were going. And then the horn began to sound.

15

Cathy Davis was working late once again. There was a new exhibition opening up at the nature museum, and she wanted to be sure that she had properly catalogued, for insurance purposes, all of the items that would be on display.

The lights had started to flicker about an hour ago, and she'd seen two security guards heading off to check the electrical boxes in the basement.

The museum was suddenly plunged into darkness. Cathy cursed to herself as she waited for the back-up generator system to kick in. This system was vital to the museum to ensure that no exhibits were endangered when there was a power failure.

She breathed a sigh of relief as the back-up generators kicked in. But her relief was short-lived as she noticed the contents of her work bench had been ransacked during the power outage. Every specimen that she had already catalogued had been dumped haphazardly in a pile.

There was a knife she didn't recognize impaled

in the top of the pile.

It looked almost like a warning.

16

Jim Evans and his crew had spent approximately seven hours at the old mill, and although it was only 7 PM, the winter darkness had already descended.

Time to call it a day. He began dismantling their equipment while waiting for a member of his team to return from the visitors' washroom. As he started to unplug the audio recording equipment, it suddenly registered a sound just as the video screen leaped to life, and a blurred shape materialized in the nearest window.

Jim retrieved his laser pointer from his briefcase, aiming it at the window and the figure reflected there. The image dissolved into a thousand points of light and then reassembled into the distinct shape of a young woman before it faded entirely.

Later Jim would discover that the video equipment had captured the woman's outline. The sound recorded on the audio equipment was indistinct. He thought he could just barely detect the word *husband.*

17

Lloyd Sumner poured himself a glass of wine as he sat in front of his big screen TV, watching a Senators' hockey game. They'd had such a promising start to their season, but were losing most of their games lately.

Lloyd was having a lot of trouble concentrating on the game. He kept thinking of Erin's gasp as she watched the footage of the antique dolls. He felt ashamed he hadn't admitted it, but he'd also seen the doll's tears.

I'll be glad when this assignment is over. Muriel Spears has selected the footage she wants. All that's left is the voice-over, and I'm out of there.

Lloyd looked up just as the Montreal Canadiens scored their second goal of the first period. The Senators were already down 2-0.

I know the feeling, guys, Lloyd thought, as he poured himself another glass of wine.

18

Sarah Bennett stood outside the old jail, waiting for the stragglers in her tour group to catch up. Although it was off-season, she was sometimes called in to lead tour groups that had requested a showing.

"I guess this would be a lot scarier around Halloween," one of the women in the group commented as she caught up to Sarah, "but unfortunately we won't be here then. Our husbands are at a conference right now," she added by way of explanation.

Sarah forced a smile. "Don't worry, this place is really scary, even in winter."

"Oh, I do hope so. I've got to have something to tell my bridge club when I get back to New Jersey."

The other members of the group had joined them so Erin led the way into the building, giving her usual spiel on the history of the jail and its famous inmate who had been charged with the murder of a Father of Confederation. No one in the group of American tourists knew what the term meant, so Erin described how four provinces had come together to form Canada in 1867. She explained that the "fathers" of Confederation were those who had shepherded the process.

She was in the middle of this explanation when one of the ladies shrieked loudly.

"What's wrong?" Sarah asked, thinking the tourist had probably lost her footing on the ice-covered concrete.

"There!!!"

As she looked where the woman was pointing, Sarah saw what appeared to be a man staring from a window. It was the execution room with the working model of the noose once used to hang prisoners.

When she saw the flare of a flashlight, Sarah realized that what she and the member of the tour group had mistaken as a man was the shadow cast by a security guard making his rounds.

Somehow, this realization didn't make her feel any better.

19

A week after the incident with the doll at the museum, Erin was consolidating her research at home. She would spend another two days at the canal museum to review the last of the documents she needed before moving on to the National Archives building on Wellington Street.

Lost in thought, she suddenly realized that her phone was ringing. She didn't recognize the number and was going to let it go to voice mail when, on a whim, she decided to answer it.

"Erin, hi, it's Lloyd Sumner. I met you at the museum. I got your number from Muriel Spears. I hope I'm not interrupting you."

"No worries, Lloyd. How's it going with the videotape?"

There was a pause at the other end. "We've just finished the voice-over, and Muriel seems happy with it and wants to send the film on to the tourism people. That will be the end of my commitment. I've already lined up another assignment. But, um, listen, could we meet for a coffee somewhere? I'd really like to talk to you about the film."

They made arrangements to meet at a local Starbucks that afternoon. As Erin walked into the coffee shop, she saw Lloyd wave to her from a corner table. She smiled, ordered a latte, and then joined him at the table.

"Thank you for coming. It took me a long time to work up the nerve to call you. This project at the museum has really gotten under my skin. I saw your reaction to the doll exhibit when I showed the footage to Muriel. I really need to know what you saw on the screen."

Erin replied hesitantly, "Well, I thought I saw one of the dolls weeping and, believe it or not, when I left the museum that night, I went to that display and discovered the doll's face and clothing were damp, as if from tears. Crazy, I know. Especially since the videotaping was done much earlier."

Lloyd heaved a long sigh of relief. "Well, if you're going crazy, we both are. When I first reviewed that footage, I saw one of the dolls move, and it seemed to be staring right at me. And when I watched the film with you and Muriel, I saw what you did: one of the dolls was crying."

"But why wouldn't Muriel see it too? I don't understand—"

"I don't really know. Maybe some people are more susceptible to these things than others. Muriel's been the curator there for so long that she's probably got every item in that place memorized.

That's what makes her good at her job. So she sees only what she's used to seeing. I know that's a stretch, but I can't think of any other way to explain it.

"And if we can see it, that means others will too. I don't think that's going to be much of an enticement for tourists if we scare the heck out of them. Unless they're part of the haunted tours, in which case I guess creepy dolls would fit right in. Kind of like the Robert and Annabelle dolls."

Erin looked confused.

"Sorry, I sometimes forget that not everyone shares my interest in cult horror films. Robert is an actual doll. It's in a Florida museum right now. The doll is supposed to be haunted: before it was placed in the museum, it talked, roamed from window to window of the house when its owner wasn't there, and had distinct facial movements, according to many people who observed it. Chucky in the *Child's Play* franchise was based on Robert the doll. And then there's the rag doll Annabelle that's supposed to be possessed by demons. They made *The Conjuring* and *Annabelle* movies based on that doll."

"Chucky, I do know. My husband took me to a horrorfest movie marathon on campus when we were undergraduates. Chucky was there, along with Freddy Kreuger, and all the other undying villains. And I remember seeing the trailers on TV for the Annabelle doll movies."

"What does your husband make of all this? I

mean the dolls at the museum?"

"Actually, they're only part of a bunch of other weird things that are happening to me there." Erin gave him a brief update on the other incidents. "He knows that I'm not prone to imagining stuff, so I think he's worried."

They ordered more coffee and then spent several more minutes hashing over their options regarding the videotape. They didn't come up with a solution, but agreed to keep in touch with each other.

20

Erin had fallen asleep at her desk in the canal museum. There was a sudden pounding overhead, and the casing of a smoke detector fell abruptly on the desk, startling her awake. She heard some giggling, and then saw a doll—the one from Lloyd's videotape—in the corner of the room. Suddenly, the doll's expression froze in a look of terror. It pointed to a shadow in the opposite corner of the room and screamed, "Help me!"

Erin woke up suddenly, realizing that she had been dreaming. She tried to will her limbs to move, but they wouldn't obey.

Seth awoke to the voice of his wife beside him. She was emitting a sound almost like a keening. Gently, he touched her shoulder.

For the second time, Erin startled awake. With an incredible sense of relief, she realized that she was no longer in the throes of the nightmare. She hugged Seth, and he saw that she'd been crying.

"Nightmare," she explained.

"It much have been an incredibly bad one.

You were making a strange sound and you've been crying."

He rocked her gently in his arms until she fell back to sleep.

21

Seth sat in his university office, tiredly rubbing his eyes. He hadn't slept much after Erin had finally drifted off to sleep. He needed more coffee. He had thirty undergraduate essays to grade.

He'd read about ten of them and was beginning to despair whether any of these kids could write more than one coherent sentence now that the shorthand of texting and Facebook had taken over. The next one he picked up from the pile was Sarah Bennett's. He remembered that she had wanted to do *The Ballad of Redding Gaol* because of her experience as a tour guide at the old Ottawa jail.

He began to read the essay:

The Ballad of Redding Gaol *has none of the playfulness and satire of Oscar Wilde's better-known works such as* The Importance of Being Earnest. *It is a poem he wrote after his release from imprisonment in Redding Gaol, where he was sentenced to two years' hard labour because of his homosexual relationship with the son of the Marquis of Queensberry. Wilde was a broken man when he left prison, and he died within two years of his release. His ballad tells the story of the execution by hanging of a fellow prisoner. It does not question the justice of the decision, but rather speaks of the commonality of suffering and despair for all prisoners....*

Seth could readily see how Sarah had been attracted to the poem. It was, of course, melodramatic and certainly not the best of Wilde's works, but it had a heartfelt openness that spoke to the reader.

He looked up as he saw movement at his office door. "Wow, talk about a coincidence. Come in, Sarah. I was just starting to read your paper. I'm enjoying it. It's very well-written."

Sarah smiled at him as she sat in his office chair. "Thanks, Professor Thomas. I'm here because I saw your notice on the bulletin board about an opening for a research assistant."

"Do you think you would be taking on too much? You already have your studies and the tour guide job."

"Actually, I quit that job. It was upsetting me too much. I don't know if I'm oversensitive or what, but I kept feeling the despair of the place, and it was getting to me. Then I started hearing and seeing things that I couldn't explain rationally."

"That's odd. My wife is going through the same thing. She's been doing research at the canal museum. For that matter, my sister has also been having strange experiences at the nature museum.

"Anyway, I'll give you a list of the research duties the job entails, and you can let me know what you think and whether it'll be too much in terms of your course load."

Sarah took the list, saying she would get back to him. She started to leave, and then turned back from the door. "This will probably sound odd, but could I possibly meet with your wife and sister? Just to compare notes."

Seth was taken aback by the request. He hesitated for a moment and then said, "Write down your phone number and e-mail address and I'll run it by them."

22

One more night, one more night. It had become her silent mantra.

Erin was getting ready for her last visit to the canal museum. Tonight she would double-check all of the references for her bibliography and look at two additional documents she'd found relating to the construction of the Rideau Canal. She grabbed her scarf—it was minus 20 Celsius with a wind chill factor that made it feel like minus 32.

Some day I'll move some place warmer, she thought, as she hurried out of the apartment. Seth was waiting for her in the car.

Seth kissed her when they arrived at the museum. "I'll text you later to see when you can come home. Stay out of trouble, okay."

"Hey, it's not my fault. Tell that to the ghost, whoever it is."

Erin unlocked the door with her key card and flicked on the overhead lights. It was already almost dark outside, although the days were very slowly getting a little bit longer, or so the weatherman on the local Ottawa TV station had assured his listeners.

There was an air of expectancy in the museum tonight, Erin thought, as if it had been awaiting her last visit.

Silly thought. I just got here and I'm already spooked.

She took the stairs up to her office on the fourth floor, removed her coat, and started to settle in. She estimated that she could finish in three hours with no distractions.

It took about two hours to verify the entries for her bibliography, and then she turned to the two remaining documents. The first was a passenger list for one of the ships that had carried canal workers from Ireland to Canada. She smiled at the frequency of the surname *Murphy* in the list. Some of these workers might in fact have been her ancestors. She and her mother were still working to complete their family tree. The second document appeared to be a death certificate, but she couldn't make out the name on it because the ink was faded.

Slowly from the third floor came the sound of keening, and she felt the hairs rise on the nape of her neck.

It's your imagination, it's your imagination. This had become her other mantra.

The sound subsided.

Good. I'm not going downstairs to investigate. I'm going to stay here and finish my work.

There was the loud bang of a door that made

her jump.

What now?

She thought she could hear footsteps moving up the stairs. She froze. Then there was the sound of whimpering, as if an animal were seeking out its master.

All sounds stopped as suddenly as they started.

Erin's hands were shaking. She closed up her laptop and prepared to put the documentation away. She planned to clean up the office and then call Seth to pick her up.

She went to the kitchen to wash out her coffee cup and replace it in the cupboard. She was feeling almost obsessive-compulsive as she performed each step of the cleaning process and suddenly found herself moving a dish cloth in aimless circles on the kitchen counter. She looked at her watch. Somehow she had lost about twenty minutes performing a simple task—as if she had experienced some type of fugue.

She forced herself to return to her office to retrieve her wastepaper basket so she could empty it in the garbage can in the kitchen. She was on her way back to the kitchen when she happened to look down at the contents of the wastepaper basket. Inside there was a pair of the white cotton gloves she used to examine fragile archive documents.

The gloves were covered in blood.

She flung the trash in the garbage can and rushed to gather up her coat and laptop.

She would call Seth from outside the museum. Better to brave the freezing temperature than to stay in this place another minute.

Part 2

The Gathering

23

After her last night at the canal museum, Erin had contacted Sarah Bennett to make arrangements to meet with her, and she'd also invited her sister-in-law Cathy and Lloyd Sumner to the meeting. Jim Evans—as yet unknown to them—would join the group later.

They met in Erin and Seth's apartment with Seth also sitting in. Following the introductions, Erin seated everyone in the living room, feeling self-conscious at the lack of space. She passed out drinks and snacks and then invited Sarah to tell her story.

"I recently left my part-time job as a tour guide, but I'd worked there for two years," Sarah began, " so I'm aware of the 'haunts' in Ottawa. For me, it was just a way of supplementing my scholarship for my undergrad studies.

"I quit about two weeks ago. It started with just small things—unexplained noises like sighs and weeping—and then it moved to physical items being displaced—tour pamphlets and maps, small giveaways we had for the tourists, and various sets of keys. I could never keep track of them from one tour to the next. It escalated with the door to one of the cells suddenly slamming shut on a visitor, and rotted bed clothing appearing in other cells.

"On my last tour, I thought I saw a man at a window in the execution room. It turned out to be a shadow, but it was enough for me. I suddenly had such a cloying sense of despair that it overwhelmed me. I don't want to ever go back there."

There was an uncomfortable silence in the room. Erin tried to lighten the mood by asking who'd like to go next. "Maybe we should call this Ghosts Anonymous: 'Hello, my name is Erin, and I'm seeing things.' " Everyone laughed politely and it helped dispel some of the tension in the room.

"How about if I go next," Erin said, "and then I'll ask Lloyd to add his comments, if that's okay with him." Lloyd nodded.

"I've been doing research in the canal museum for about a month now. For me, it started with a vague sense of malaise. I would hear sounds, get strange calls on my cellphone, and discover objects displaced, like Sarah mentioned. The last visit there, I found a pair of my cotton gloves in a wastepaper basket. They were bloodied. And one of the most frightening experiences—aside from the dolls, which Lloyd will explain—was almost being pushed down a flight of stairs. I could have sworn that I felt someone's hand in the small of my back."

Seth interjected at this point to mention that

both Erin and Cathy were experiencing nightmares. He asked if Lloyd and Sarah were also suffering from sleep disturbances, but they both shook their heads.

Erin continued. "One of the strangest experiences has been with the dolls. I'll let Lloyd take over from here."

Lloyd, looking slightly mortified at being called upon to speak, as if remembering his public speaking disasters in high school, said: "Um, I'm a videographer. I had a contract to film the museum for the upcoming tourist season. Erin was there the day I did the filming. When I started reviewing the film back at my apartment, everything was fine until I got to the museum's display of antique dolls. I was sure I saw one of them move and stare straight at me, but then I ran the film again several times, and couldn't see any movement."

He paused to take a drink of pop and then continued. "I figured I was imagining this, but when I showed the film to the curator of the museum, Erin was with us. When it came to the doll exhibit, she gasped, and she told me later that she'd seen one of the dolls weeping. I saw the same thing."

Erin then described the incident at the museum where she discovered the face and clothing of the doll to be damp. There was silence once again in the room.

"I guess it's my turn," Cathy said, as she took a sip from her wine glass. "I have a job in restoration at the nature museum and often have to work late. I've had experiences similar to the ones you've all described. The elevators are continually running without anyone operating them, there are unexplained sounds, and my tools are constantly being rearranged. In fact, the last night I worked late, I couldn't find my car keys. A security guard finally located them for me on the floor of a freight elevator. I have no idea how they got there. And, as my brother's already mentioned, I'm having trouble sleeping."

Seth spoke up. "I know these places are supposed to be haunted, but I always thought those stories were just for fun at Halloween. I mean who doesn't like a good ghost story? But what I don't understand is why all of you are experiencing these incidents. What's the common thread?"

Erin volunteered to do more research to explore the linkages. "I'm doing historical research for my thesis so it won't be too far astray for me."

They agreed to meet again once they heard back from Erin.

After they left, Erin turned to Seth with a troubled expression. "I hope this is the right thing to do. I mean, Sarah is your student, and if word of our meeting gets out, it could jeopardize your work at Carleton. And what about your sister? I'm not sure the nature museum's board of directors would look kindly upon having a staff member who thinks she's being hounded by ghosts."

"I know there are risks, Erin, but I think we should deal with the issue. Neither you nor Cathy is sleeping, and Sarah's deeply troubled—it's obvious just to look at her. And Lloyd seems very unsure what to make of all this."

"Okay," Erin conceded. "I'll go ahead with the research. And I think maybe I should call Martha and ask her to speak to her friend. I'll call now before I lose my nerve."

Erin made the call to Martha.

"Martha speaking. George is busy writing his memoirs."

Erin laughed. "What are you going to do when you run out of 'Martha' jokes?"

"No problem, I'll just switch to my last name. I had a feeling you'd be calling. How're you doing, kiddo?"

"Well, if there's comfort in numbers, then I guess I'm feeling slightly reassured that I'm not the only one going crazy." Erin went on to describe the group meeting and how the incidents were occurring at three different locations."

"Surely there must be links."

"Well, I know that the plaster cast of Thomas D'Arcy McGee's hand is in the canal museum and that his convicted murderer was hanged in the old jail on Nicholas Street. But I haven't been able to make the link with the nature museum where Cathy works. I'm going to do more research and see what I come up with. In the meantime, I think I'll take you up on your offer and meet with the friend you mentioned. The one, um, with the psychic abilities."

"Jeez, you make it sound like she has the clap or something. She's actually very reputable. But I need to check with her and tell her what's up so she can decide whether she'll be able to help you. I'll call her in the morning and get back to you. Her name, by the way, is Eva Maynard."

Erin thanked her and ended the call. She immediately opened her laptop and googled the name Martha had given her.

24

Eva Maynard was a woman in her late sixties, short and heavy-set. She wore her long grey hair in a tight bun. With her granny glasses, she looked like a grandmother who should be knitting socks. But she was also fiercely intelligent and had a quick awareness that allowed her to sum up a situation within minutes. She would have made an excellent detective.

Eva had a *gift* (or *curse*, as she sometimes thought of it) that had been passed down from generation to generation in her matrilineal ancestry. It had been called many things: sixth sense, second sight, ESP, empathy, psychic power, ghost whispering, and even witchcraft in earlier times. She preferred to use the term *sensitive* to describe herself. Spirits left behind on earth came to her without her bidding. Sometimes they were benign; sometimes they were tricksters; and sometimes they were dangerous. But they all wanted one thing: to cross over from this earth to whatever awaited them on the other side.

As she spoke to Martha Bellows on the phone that morning, she said: "You know, Martha, I don't perform parlour tricks, and I don't do this for money. Make sure they know that. I won't be mocked for my gift. If they're serious about this and genuinely need my help, then this Erin you spoke of can contact me."

Martha laughed. "Eva, do you know how many times you've given me that spiel? Relax. You know I take you very seriously. And these people *definitely* could use your help."

"Okay. You can give Erin my number. But make sure she knows I can't guarantee I'll be able to help her and her friends."

25

Erin had found nothing of substance on the internet relating to Eva Maynard, other than a mention or two in reports of a local paranormal investigation group. From what she could tell, Mrs. Maynard assisted this group from time to time in their investigations.

In the meantime, Martha had called to give her Mrs. Maynard's number. For several minutes, Erin fingered the slip of paper on which she'd written the number, then heaved a sigh, and made the phone call.

Eva Maynard answered on the third ring.

"Oh, hello, Mrs. Maynard. This is Erin Murphy. Martha gave me your number and said you'd be expecting my call."

"Hi, Erin. Please call me Eva. Yes, Martha's spoken to me of the experiences of you and your friends. If I understand correctly, you're at a bit of an impasse. You don't know what to make of these incidents, but they're still affecting all of you in one way or another. Tell me, Erin, how long has it been since your last visit to the canal museum? I understand you've been doing research there."

"It was about two weeks ago. I've finished my research there now, so I don't really need to go back, but the museum is about to open for Winterlude and that's making me feel uncomfortable." She was referring to the annual winter festival in Ottawa that attracted throngs of tourists.

"Do you still have access to the museum, Erin?"

"Yes, I do. I was going to turn in my key card last week to the curator, but I was busy and forgot."

"Are you allowed to bring anyone with you when you use your pass? I'm not sure what arrangement you have with the museum."

"Yes, I'm a member of the historical society that supports the museum, and I'm listed as a researcher. I can have someone accompany me. Martha went in with me when I first started my research. She'd never been inside and wanted to explore the museum when no tourists were there. In fact, she was badly spooked by the place and left shortly after she got there."

"If you're agreeable, I'd like to have you take me as a guest to the museum to get a feel for the place. Sometimes I'm capable of sensing presences. Other times, I'm not. I can go tomorrow evening, if that's not too short a notice."

"Not at all. I'd be happy to show it to you."

That's a bit of an exaggeration. I never, ever wanted to go into that building again.

And now I have to.

26

The following evening, Erin picked Eva up at her apartment and they drove together to the museum. As Erin parked the car and they walked toward the building, Eva said: "I know it's hard, but could you pretend I'm not here and go ahead with the routine you followed when you were doing your research? I'll just be walking around. I may touch a wall or the top of a display case, but I promise not to disturb anything."

"Yes, of course," Erin agreed as she opened the door to the museum and took their coats to hang up. "Okay, I usually work upstairs if the documents I'm using can be removed from the archives. The curator set up a small office for me up there."

"Go ahead upstairs then, Erin. I'll call you if I find anything of interest."

Erin went upstairs as Eva began looking at the various displays. The first floor of the museum was devoted to exhibits related to the building of the Rideau Canal, a feat accomplished in six years with "navvies" working only with hand tools. Looking at these photos, you did not have to be a sensitive to know that there were many sad stories behind the grim faces depicted there.

Eva stopped at a display that featured a bust and painting of Colonel By. Sensing nothing there, she decided to move on. The second floor housed artifacts relating to the early days of Bytown. She paused by the exhibit showing the lumber barons and then moved to the photographs of the timber rafts navigating the Ottawa River.

Eva saved the doll exhibit for last. There were many Victorian-era memorabilia—toys, games, and household devices among them.

She stopped as she heard a sound—almost like one child shushing another. And in the background was the sound of weeping.

Eva's immediate reaction was so strong that she clutched her heart and her legs went limp.

Erin found her lying slumped on the floor several minutes later. She had gone to investigate why Eva had not responded when she'd called down to her. For a brief moment, Erin was terribly afraid that Eva was dead.

Eva Maynard heard someone calling her name—as if from a long way off—and then saw Erin Murphy leaning over her, looking terrified. Eva remembered the weeping before she collapsed on the floor. She started to get up, but Erin told her to stay until she brought a chair over.

"It's okay, Erin, really it is. Hazard of the trade,

I'm afraid," Eva said as Erin helped her to the chair and brought her some water to drink. "This has happened to me a couple of times before. It's as if the emotion I'm experiencing overwhelms me physically. I just need some rest. Could you please take me home now?"

Erin drove Eva home and helped her settle into her apartment. "Are you sure you don't need me to call someone to be with you?"

"I'm fine, Erin. I'm just going to have a cup of tea and then go to bed. But thank you for being so concerned."

Erin left reluctantly, promising to call Eva in the morning to see how she was feeling.

After Erin left, Eva turned on her electric kettle and sat down heavily in a kitchen chair. Despite her assurances to Erin, she was badly shaken. The last time this had happened to her two years ago, she'd been hospitalized, and the doctors had advised her that she'd suffered a mild heart attack. She would need to decide if she had the strength to continue with this investigation.

As she drifted off to sleep that night, Eva was vaguely aware of the room growing colder. She had a strange dream. There was a young woman in the centre of a group of children. The children were circling her and chanting "ring-around-the-rosie." When they reached the part of the refrain that went "ashes, ashes," they fell down with their arms outstretched over the woman.

It was not clear whether they were protecting or attacking her.

27

Erin awoke to the sound of her phone ringing. It was almost 9:00 AM, and Seth had already left for the university. She had slept in, a rare treat for her. When she answered, she recognized Eva's voice.

"I hope I didn't wake you. I know you promised to call, but I'm going out to meet a friend. I didn't want you to worry when you didn't get an answer. I'm afraid I'm terribly old-fashioned. All I have is my phone at home. What do the young people call it these days? Oh, right. A land line. Anyway, I just wanted to let you know that I'm feeling much better."

They talked for a few minutes, and Erin was pleased to hear the older woman's voice sounding much stronger than it had last night. They ended the conversation with an agreement to wait a week before continuing with their investigation.

Eva Maynard's friend was already sitting at a table when she entered the coffee shop. She smiled at him, got a cup of tea at the counter, and then joined him. "Good to see you again, Jim. It's been awhile. Last year, I think, when you called me in to help you with the Grant House. How have you been?"

Jim Evans smiled affectionately at Eva Maynard. He normally did not work with psychics in his paranormal investigations because he found they could distract his team by focusing exclusively on specific "hot spots" of paranormal activity rather than examining the site as a whole. But this was not the case with Eva. He had relied on her a few times in the past when his clients had specifically requested that a psychic be present. He was very fond of her and had great respect for her abilities.

"Good to see you, Eva. I'm doing fine. Just finished up at the old Manotick mill. We got some interesting audio and video that we're analyzing. What have you been up to?"

Eva explained her current undertaking with Erin Murphy and her group. She then told him what had happened the previous evening at the canal museum.

Jim was immediately concerned. "I thought something was bothering you when you called and asked to meet me. I really don't think it's a good idea for you to pursue this investigation, Eva. You must have someone you can trust who will take over for you."

"Yes, I do. And I'm looking at him right now."

"I'm flattered, Eva, but I don't have any of your abilities as a sensitive. All I do is try to record evidence of paranormal events when I'm invited in."

"I know, Jim. But hear me out. I thought I'd let you take the lead on this, if you have the time. You can spearhead the investigation, and I'll review any evidence you find. Hopefully, at second remove I won't be so vulnerable to whatever it is that I encountered last night."

After much back and forth, Jim reluctantly agreed to meet with Erin's group to discuss this new arrangement.

"I'll give her a call, and she can set up a meeting with you. Thanks again, Jim. There may be no danger for me, but I don't want to risk another heart attack." She touched his hand and gathered up her coat and purse to leave. Her apartment was within walking distance.

Jim sat back, finished his coffee, and prepared to leave. He smiled as he put on his jacket.

Good old Eva. I never could say no to her.

28

The following week Jim Evans joined the group in Erin's apartment. The other members were hesitant at first to discuss their experiences, but they gradually relaxed. He was adept at putting people at ease, a skill that had always come naturally to him.

"So, if I understand this correctly, there are three distinct locations for these experiences and you're not sure if or how they are related. I guess I could start with the obvious. They're all very old buildings in this city, and they have a history of being haunted. But none of you strikes me as being susceptible to haunted house stories. So you've approached this in a rational manner trying to determine what's been happening in these buildings. Cathy and Erin are related through marriage, and they both work in museums: one in a permanent position and the other for short-term research. Lloyd, you've had experiences at the canal museum as well. And Sarah, you've had some unsettling experiences while working at the old jail. Does this about sum it up?"

They all nodded in agreement.

"I've just finished an investigation at the Manotick mill, which is also an old stone building along the Rideau that has a history of being haunted. Maybe that site is related to what you've been experiencing. I certainly don't want to rule it out.

"I understand that Eva had a very strong reaction when she visited the canal museum with you, Erin. It's interesting because my team did an investigation there about three years ago, but we didn't have any findings to report."

"I remember reading about that on the internet," Erin interjected.

"Yes. We didn't experience anything out of the ordinary when we were there, but I do remember having a strong feeling of malaise with no apparent reason for it."

"Well, maybe if I talk to Muriel Spears—she's the curator—I can get you invited back," Erin said. "If you're willing to go there again," she added as an afterthought. She knew she certainly didn't want to, especially after what had happened to poor Eva.

29

Muriel Spears had been on leave when Jim Evans and his paranormal team conducted their original investigation of the canal museum. Her temporary replacement in the job had invited them in. And, at first, she balked when Erin suggested a second visit by the paranormal group.

"What is it you're not telling me, Erin? They didn't find anything the first time. What makes you think they should go back there?"

Without going into detail, Erin explained that she was very uncomfortable in the museum and thought it would be a good idea while it was closed to visitors to have Jim Evans and his team take a second look. The explanation was lame, but she knew that Muriel was a pragmatist who would probably just shake her head at Erin's stories.

Muriel narrowed her eyes thoughtfully and said, "I know there's more going on than you're telling me, Erin. But you're a respected member of the historical society, and I certainly don't think you're given to flights of fancy. Go ahead and tell this Jim Evans that I've approved the visit, but tell him I don't want the video showing up on YouTube. Haunted houses may play well at Halloween, but I'd prefer having our museum known for its preservation of Ottawa's history."

Erin agreed and told Muriel that she would take responsibility for the visit and ensure that nothing in the museum was disturbed. "I think they'll want to go within the next few days."

"Okay, but keep me posted on the outcome."

Jim Evans's plan was to investigate the two museums and the former jail, and then to return to the Manotick mill. He had a feeling that such a visit would somehow close the circle, although *what* circle he didn't know and *why* he felt that way he couldn't explain. He was anxious to get started and so was very pleased when he got the okay for the canal museum visit.

Two days later, he and his team were escorted into the museum by Erin. They set up their audio and video equipment, and then said good-bye to her. They preferred to investigate without others present so they could be as objective as possible. Erin readily agreed to leave. She did so with a huge sigh of relief.

30

It was 6 PM, and they had been in the canal museum for almost three hours. Jim had detected several cold spots, verified through a thermometer, although he knew that a building this old would potentially have drafts. Normally, he was very calm at these investigations, but this time he felt agitated and anxious. He observed that the other members of his team also appeared to be on edge and were uncharacteristically quiet. No one talked to pass the time. No one touched the snacks he'd distributed.

It started innocuously enough. They thought they saw a flash in the large mirror they'd set up on the ground floor. Then there was an irritating noise from the audio recorder.

And then all hell broke loose.

The chanting arose from somewhere overhead:

Ashes, ashes,
We all fall down.

Next came the keening sound, and the walls of the building itself poured water as if weeping.

Then all of the electrical equipment began to malfunction at once. And objects were flung across the room.

Afterward their accounts of what happened would differ slightly, but would have a common underlying element.

Fear.

31

After their audio and visual equipment had become useless, Jim Evans and his team waited an hour to see if there would be any further incidents. They felt the stone walls inch by inch, but there was no evidence of moisture. They decided to pack up their equipment and leave. Jim invited the others to his apartment to see if they'd captured anything on their equipment before it had malfunctioned.

The other members of his team, Keisha, Robert, and Stephen, were devoted professionals. Like Jim, they had full-time jobs, but they'd joined his paranormal investigation team because of his reputation for objectivity and thoroughness. They sat now in his living room, drinking whisky on the rocks and trying to relax. Jim had asked them to spend the night, and they had all gratefully accepted.

Keisha, the oldest of the investigators and a newspaper editor in her regular job, spoke first: "What the hell just happened?"

Robert added, "I kept trying to take everything

in but it was sensory overload."

The others nodded in agreement.

Jim got up to scrounge some supper for them, using the time to try to distance himself from what had happened. He poured some stale Doritos into a large bowl, cut the mould off a chunk of cheddar cheese he'd found buried at the back of the fridge and sliced it on a paper plate, and then nuked some day-old pizza. A veritable feast.

As he put the plates out on his coffee table, he realized that the adrenaline spike from their fight-or-flight response at the museum had ended, and they were all ravenous. They gratefully devoured the food and then decided to call out for more pizza. While they waited, Robert and Stephen, the team's electronic gurus, examined their equipment to see if the circuits were fried.

Stephen managed to get the audio equipment functioning again, but it had recorded only a high-pitched whine similar to what Erin had heard on her cell phone. The video equipment—when resurrected—showed nothing out of the ordinary.

Then Keisha looked up suddenly as if she'd just remembered something. "Wait. Before everything went sideways, I was taking some footage on my digital camera. It's battery-operated so it shouldn't have been affected."

She reached into her over-sized purse and withdrew the camera. Jim noticed that her hands were shaking badly.

They examined the still images on the camera. Keisha had somehow managed to take three photos. In the first photo, there was a dark, amorphous spectre reflected in the floor-length mirror they'd set up in the museum. By the third photo, the spectre had assumed the shape of a woman dressed in black.

They jumped involuntarily as the intercom sounded, and then felt sheepish when they realized it was only the pizza delivery man.

32

Eva looked troubled as she examined the digital photos that Jim had downloaded to her computer.

"It looks like the grieving woman from my dream. I guess that would account for the keening sounds you heard and the weeping. In my dream she was encircled by children. They were chanting the ring-around-the-rosie rhyme. And you say you heard that chant before your equipment malfunctioned?"

"Yes, all of us did. What do you sense, Eva? There's obviously sorrow, but is there anything else?"

"Let me review them one by one. Can you zoom in on each photo?" She examined them minutely until she thought the individual pixels would explode in her head.

They both saw it at the same time. In the corner of the third photograph was a doll that had been displaced from its exhibit. But the doll wasn't crying. It looked directly at the screen and seemed to smirk, as if at a slow student who was taking much too long to solve an easy puzzle.

After his meeting with Eva, Jim contacted Erin and Lloyd to show them the photograph with the doll. They stared at the enlarged computer image Jim had downloaded on Erin's laptop.

"It's the same doll I saw in the videotape I made," Lloyd said.

Erin concurred. "I saw it in the videotape screening for Muriel and later I found moisture on its face and costume in the museum. But it's different this time. It's as if something has emboldened it or maybe given it hope. I don't know how else to express it."

"Erin, do you know anything about the doll's provenance?" Jim queried.

"Yes, I did some research. It's mid- to late-nineteenth century so I don't think it could be related to a canal death. The canal was fully constructed before then. Unless—"

Jim finished her thought. "Unless it's been drawn into this whole circle of events, as we have."

33

The following week, Cathy Davis met Jim Evans in the atrium of the nature museum. By mutual consent, they had settled on Jim visiting the museum by himself rather than making a formal request to the museum directors for a paranormal investigation by his team. They agreed that given the red tape involved, it would probably take months before the request was even considered. Also, Jim didn't want to jeopardize Cathy's job. He knew from experience that a lot of people didn't take well to talk of the supernatural.

"Hi, Jim. Thanks so much for coming. Most of the fossils I restore end up in the fossil gallery on the main floor so I thought you'd probably want to start there."

Jim agreed. "I've had a look at the gallery on the website's virtual tour. It's amazing—the size and diversity of the collection. I think I can safely say that I'll need at least the morning here.

I know there's a café in back. Could I buy you lunch?"

"That would be nice. How about I meet you there around noon?"

After agreeing to meet Cathy for lunch, Jim started exploring the fossil gallery. Cathy's work, she had told him, involved the identification of specimens, and she was also responsible for their conservation and restoration, where necessary. He didn't have Eva Maynard's sensitivity to emotions, but what he was looking for was more tangible: he was hoping to discover a nexus between this museum and the other venues.

He spent the morning looking at the various reconstructed specimens on display: most of them were immense dinosaurs that towered hundreds of feet above him. He also read the information about each specimen and was tired and ready for lunch by noon.

Cathy was waiting for him outside the entrance to the café, and together they found a corner table.

"How was your morning?" Cathy inquired. "This museum can be quite overwhelming. There's so much here."

Jim laughed. "Yes, I'm discovering that. And I'm only at ground level."

"Usually, it takes several visits to do justice to the whole of the museum. And there are also some visiting exhibits on display right now on the Arctic ecosystem."

Jim had a sudden thought. "Is it possible that the canal museum shared displays with this facility at some time in the past? Or that they sent fossils or other specimens here for identification?"

Cathy considered this suggestion. "Yes, it's certainly possible. In fact, there have been various times when construction in Ottawa has unearthed bones—both human and animal—so some specimens may have been sent here. I'm not sure where to start, but I can try to find something in our computerized inventory. The specimens would certainly have been logged into the museum's database. I usually work late so maybe this evening I can have a look."

"Thanks, Cathy. I have to head back to my day job after I finish eating"—he worked for the federal government as a statistical analyst—"but you can reach me any time by phone or text." He gave her his cell phone number, and she smiled to herself.

"What? What's so amusing?"

She looked embarrassed. "Sorry, I was just thinking that it's been a long time since a man's given me his number."

"I find that very surprising. I'll look forward to your call."

Cathy returned to her workstation. After her regular shift ended, she began searching the museum's databases. It was nearing 8 PM, and she'd found nothing. She finally came upon a section entitled "excavation transfers" and impatiently waded through a list of specimens sent to the museum from Canadian universities. She backtracked when she saw Carleton University in the list and then read the description of the artifact they had sent for analysis:

> *Bone fragment measuring 25 cm (10 inches) by 15.24 cm (6 inches), badly deteriorated, excavated in Ottawa burial ground (c. 1820-1870), human (?), sent for DNA testing.*

Cathy knew instinctively that this was the link they were looking for.

She reached for her phone.

34

Eva Maynard was watering an amaryllis plant that she'd grown from a bulb, a Christmas gift from a friend, when the doorbell rang. She put down the watering can, peered out the window, and saw Jim Evans standing on her doorstep.

"Come in, Jim. It's freezing out there. What brings you out on such a cold day?"

Jim removed his boots at the door, and then entered the living room. Eva gestured him to a chair. "Sorry for just barging in, Eva, but I need to run something by you. I don't know if you can get any kind of reading off a photograph, but unfortunately it's all I have." He withdrew the photograph from his briefcase. "The item's in the DNA lab at the nature museum, and it can't be removed."

"Wait, I need my glasses ... oh, here they are." She ran her fingers over the specimen of bone in the photograph. At first, she felt nothing. Then in her mind she saw a dark shape take form. She gasped and sat down shakily. It was the woman in mourning clothes from her dream.

Seeing her agitation, Jim rose to get her a glass of water from the kitchen. "I'm sorry it upset you, Eva. What was it you saw?"

Eva gratefully accepted the glass of water and took several small sips before she answered. "I saw a woman dressed in mourning clothes. I've seen her before in my dream, and I think she was the spectre you glimpsed at the canal museum.

"But this time I saw something else ... the doll from the museum ... the same as in the digital photo you showed me. Except that it had the same countenance as the grieving woman. And the doll was crying too."

35

Erin was sitting in a cubicle at the National Archives building. She'd spent every free moment in the past two weeks there and was finally starting to see her research take shape. She'd met with her thesis adviser the previous week to show him a draft outline, and he'd been very pleased with it. She was now filling in gaps to make sure she had all of the information she needed.

Erin stretched to take a kink from her back. She would have to start exercising again soon, she realized. All of this sitting was getting to her. Maybe the exercise would help her sleep better as well.

Her cell phone vibrated. It was a text from Jim Evans asking her to call him that evening.

****

Later, when she was eating supper with Seth in their apartment, he commented, "You still seem down, Erin. Want to talk about it?" He realized that he'd seldom seen his wife laugh or smile in the past two months.

"Oh, that reminds me. I'm supposed to call Jim Evans. He sent me a text this afternoon." She dried her hands on a kitchen towel, and went to find her cell phone.

"I'm no psychiatrist, Erin, but from my Psych 101 course way back when, I'd say you're using avoidance techniques because you don't want to talk about what's bothering you," Seth replied.

"Let me call Jim and see if he has any news, and then we can sit and talk about it. You know how on edge I get when I'm overtired. Maybe it's just that."

Seth wasn't convinced that it was simply a matter of Erin being overtired, but he didn't say anything more.

Erin entered Jim's number, and he answered on the first ring. "Thanks for returning my call, Erin. I'd like to set up another meeting with you and your group. We can meet at my apartment. Maybe a change in venue would be good."

He explained what Cathy had discovered and Eva's subsequent reaction to the photograph.

"I think we're looking at the ghost of a grieving relative, but I want to run it by the group to see where to take this."

They agreed to meet on the weekend, and Erin began calling the others as soon as she ended her conversation with Jim.

Still avoiding our talk, Seth thought.

They never did discuss what was bothering Erin. Instead she'd taken a shower and fallen asleep on their bed. Seth kissed her forehead as he covered her with a quilt. She felt unusually warm.

Maybe there's something physical at the base of this.

In her dream, Erin was skating on the Rideau Canal. It was nearing dusk, and she was alone. The temperature had grown warmer, and there were soft spots in the ice. Her skate blade hit one of the spots and she fell. The ice around her began to break. Suddenly a hand reached out, pulling her into the endless dark water below.

Seth was marking essays in the living room, and was lost in thought when he heard Erin's scream. He ran to comfort her, feeling his inadequacy in dealing with whatever was happening to his wife.

36

On Friday night, Jim Evans greeted Erin and the other members of her group and invited them into his apartment. Once everyone was settled, he asked Cathy to bring them up-to-date regarding the specimen she'd uncovered.

"Jim suggested to me that maybe the canal museum had loaned a display to my facility, so I started doing research online. I discovered that Carleton University had sent a specimen to the nature museum for DNA analysis. We have that new state-of-the-art lab so we get a lot of referrals. Anyway, the bone fragment was from an excavation site. Remember when that work crew dug up graves a couple of years back? Well, this bone fragment was from that site, and Jim and I agree that this must be the link we've been looking for."

Erin looked puzzled. "But if the specimen came from the university, how does it relate to the canal museum?"

"Well, it was a bit of a stretch at first. It was just something I felt instinctively. It made sense to me:

a museum devoted to the history of the building of the Rideau Canal. A bone fragment that was found in a burial spot for canal workers. Even the link to Carleton University seemed fortuitous given that you and Seth and Sarah all have ties to the university—"

"Do you know when the DNA analysis on the bone fragment will be ready, Cathy?" Lloyd inquired.

"The lab has already finished it. The bone is human, but unfortunately the identity of the person is still unknown," Cathy replied.

"That's to be expected," Erin added. "A lot of the Irish canal workers were buried without relatives to claim their bodies. And the wooden grave markers have all decayed with time."

Cathy nodded to Jim. "Maybe you can take over here and explain Eva's reaction."

"I couldn't remove the specimen, of course, but Cathy was able to photograph it, and I showed Eva the photo. She saw the same grieving woman and the doll from the canal museum. So we need to decide where to go from here."

Sarah looked puzzled. "But if all of the haunted locations are related, as we agreed at our last meeting, how do we establish a connection with the old jail? It wasn't constructed until 1862, which means that we can't be looking at the widow of a canal worker."

Erin spoke up: "When I was doing my research,

I discovered that there are about twenty burial sites along the canal. They were used for local burials for at least fifty years after the canal's construction. So the bone fragment doesn't necessarily have to belong to a canal worker."

"That means that if there's a tie-in with the old jail, we're looking for a death that occurred after 1862," Jim said. "I'm willing to visit the jail. I don't think I'll have trouble getting permission to conduct an investigation there. There's always news footage of the building on the Ottawa CTV channel every Halloween. The place seems to thrive on its history of being haunted. I'll see if I can set something up within the next two weeks."

37

Jim Evans received permission from the owners of the hostel to conduct an investigation of the former jail. It was now mid-February, and he was anxious to conclude this investigation so he could have a second go-round at the Manotick mill.

He and his team set up their equipment in the old jail building on a Tuesday afternoon. They'd received permission to use the eighth floor, which was normally off-limits to the public except during tours.

Although Jim struggled to keep an open mind, he'd already noticed the cold spots in the death row cells on this floor. A sense of despair still permeated the building despite all of the renovations done to create the new hostel.

When the old jail was still operating, it had no heat or ventilation. Confined to tiny cells, the prisoners froze in winter and sweltered in the heat of summer. For prisoners who reached this floor, there was no hope left. They were on their way to the gallows.

Jim remembered reading that hangings were

often gruesome affairs because the condemned men and women didn't always die quickly. Arthur Ellis—Canada's legendary hangman—was notorious for miscalculating the counterbalance weight to be attached to the rope. His last execution resulted in the beheading of the prisoner.

They had been at the site for a couple of hours when the audio equipment recorded activity: it sounded as if someone were praying or counting rosary beads. Or perhaps it was a priest hearing a last confession.

The slight noise was then followed by a burst of static. Jim was about to adjust the volume on the machine when his peripheral vision caught the image of a man bowed in the corner of a cell. But when he looked inside the cell, there was no one there.

After another hour, the audio machinery recorded another burst of activity. The voice this time was very low, but they could make out a few words as presumably judgment was being pronounced on a condemned prisoner:

Holden ... sentenced to hang ... God have mercy...

Static again.

Then a woman's piercing scream.

Jim was startled by a hand on his shoulder. He realized it was Keisha and that she had been calling his name several times. When he looked up at her, she held out her hand. "I have no idea where this came from, Jim. The scream startled me, and I felt something brush against my hand. When I looked down, this is what I found."

There was a frayed piece of rope entwined around her fingers. It had been fashioned into a small noose.

38

Once advised of the results of the investigation at the old jail, Erin had immediately begun to research the name Holden. She located an internet site that listed all of the persons executed in Canada before capital punishment was abolished, along with their crimes. Arthur Holden had been hanged in 1864—just two years after the jail was opened. His crime: the murder of Robert Creighton. Erin googled both names and came across a few references.

She opened and read an *Ottawa Citizen* newspaper article dated May 1863:

> *The body of Robert Creighton of no fixed address was discovered floating in the canal on Tuesday, May 17. There is speculation that Creighton fell into the river while in an inebriated state. Police are searching for any witnesses to the event. An inquest is scheduled...*

A follow-up article appeared in June:

A witness has come forth claiming he saw two men fighting and that one of them pushed the other into the canal in mid-May. The body of Robert Creighton was subsequently recovered from the canal. An inquest confirms that Creighton had been badly beaten and was most likely near death when his body was dumped...

There were three subsequent articles dealing with the arrest; trial and sentencing; and execution of Arthur Holden, who maintained his innocence throughout the trial. The prosecution had relied almost exclusively on the testimony of the witness, who was identified as Marc Jordan.

Holden admitted at trial that he was at the same pub as the victim Creighton that evening, but said that he had not talked to Creighton or seen him again after the man left the pub.

Holden was executed in the Ottawa jail, and his body was claimed by his wife Mary and buried, presumably in the site where the bone fragment had been recovered. He left behind three young children.

Erin also found a reference to Arthur Holden in a book on the history of capital punishment in Canada. The author of the book had researched the Creighton murder and questioned the credibility of Jordan's testimony. What had not come out at

Holden's trial was the fact that Jordan had perjured his testimony in a previous trial.

Okay, I see the links with the two museums and the jail, Erin thought. *But how does the Manotick mill figure in?*

She would find out soon enough.

39

It felt like déjà vu for Jim Evans and his team as they set up their equipment on the second floor of the old Manotick mill. The death of Joseph Merrill Currier's young bride Anne had occurred in 1860, pre-dating the trial and execution of Arthur Holden. If there was a link, Jim wasn't seeing it, although he remained steadfast in his belief that the death at the mill was the final piece of the puzzle.

Is the truth staring me in the face? Is it a case of Occam's razor—the simplest solution is the best one? Mary Holden lost an innocent husband to a violent death. Joseph Merrill Currier lost his innocent bride to a violent death four years earlier. Both spouses grieved their loss.

Jim was so deeply lost in thought that at first he did not see the tiny object abandoned beneath the old machinery.

But when he finally noticed it and bent to pick it up, he realized that he had the final piece of the puzzle.

40

Jim Evans sat in Eva Maynard's living room, updating her on the events in the old jail and his second visit to the Manotick mill. He shared his theory on the death of Joseph Merrill Currier's wife Anne.

"Where do you go from here, Jim? And how can I help?"

"It's silly, Eva, but I keep thinking of a line from an old song. Something about the circle being unbroken. I have no idea what that means."

Eva smiled a very sad smile. "I think I know, Jim. I think it's time for me to come back into the circle."

"I can't ask that of you, Eva. There's the threat to your health—"

"I don't think I have a choice in this matter. Not if we want to find peace."

Part 3

Reaching Out

41

They sat in a circle at a makeshift table set up in Eva's living room. On the table were the photos and items they'd amassed from the two museums, the jail, and the old Manotick mill. Erin, Cathy, Jim, and Sarah were present at Eva's request. They would advise Lloyd of the results later. As for Seth, he was waiting anxiously for his wife in Eva's kitchen. He'd been cautioned not to intervene no matter what he heard.

Eva had lit candles and was burning incense. They joined hands to form a circle. Erin and Sarah looked apprehensive, while Cathy seemed slightly amused, as if they were taking part in a scene from a B horror movie.

"I'm a sensitive. Spirits generally come to me. I don't call them forth. I've only participated in three other séances, and I think the trappings—the candles and incense—aren't really necessary. But they may help you relax a bit." She smiled at Cathy as if reading her thoughts. "They are a bit Hollywood, aren't they?

"The spirits, if they wish to be seen, will come forward. This is a strenuous process for me, and I need your support."

The other members of the circle murmured in agreement.

"We think—but don't know for sure—that we're dealing with at least two spirits: the ghost of Arthur Holden's widow Mary and that of Joseph Merrill Currier's bride Anne. But there may be more, and they may be less benevolent. Erin, I'm thinking of the entity that pushed you on the stairs and the dark presence in your dreams. If I sense any danger, I'll ask you to break the circle, and I'll stop immediately. Is that clear to everyone?" She spoke with a tone of authority.

The others nodded their heads in assent.

"I'm going to start with the photograph of the doll that Jim's fellow team member Keisha took at the canal museum because it seems to be the image we've encountered most frequently." She touched the photo, her fingers lingering on the doll's face.

Two things happened at once. There was a low keening sound from the corner of the room, and something touched Eva's shoulder. The others could see her react.

"Stay in place, all of you.

"I am trying to reach Mary Holden. Is she present in this room?"

No response. The keening stopped abruptly.

"Mary, are you present?" she asked again.

Eva could feel the cold air behind her. "I believe you are standing behind me, Mary. You have nothing to fear from any of us. We are trying to help you. Can you please come forward?"

Again nothing. Then there was movement behind Eva. She looked extremely disturbed. "I sense another presence in this room. Keep the circle for now unless I order you to break it.

"Who are you? What do you want with Mary?" Eva asked.

There was the sound of contemptuous laughter in the room. They all tensed, but kept their hands together.

A male voice said: *Old woman, I could kill you with a glance. You mean nothing to me. It's Mary's soul that I want.*

"Why do you want Mary? What has she done to you?" Eva demanded.

The male voice spoke once again: *I drowned that miscreant Robert Creighton in the canal: he owed me money and refused to pay. I framed Holden for the murder because I fancied his wife.*

You could be mine, Mary. I would cherish you forever. We could have in death what we never shared in life.

Eva interjected, "If you really love her, you will let her spirit go."

The male voice rose in anger: *Blasphemy, old woman. Do not speak of letting her go!*

Eva was about to command the others to break

the circle when a female voice spoke in a chilling tone: *You will never have me. Now that I know it was you who betrayed my husband, my children and I can cross over.*

I consign you to Hell, Jordan!!!

The male voice screamed in anguish. Then the room grew quiet.

Suddenly there was the sound of children's laughter.

A child's voice spoke: *Are we going now, Mother? Can I bring my dolly with me? She wants to go too ... Oh, thank you, Mother, thank you. Here we go, dolly.*

And then Eva asked urgently, "Is there anyone else in this room?

"Anne, departed wife of Joseph Merrill Currier, are you present? Can we assist you to cross over?"

Silence. Then another voice in the room. A different woman. She sounded much younger than Mary: *I've lost the bonnet I knitted. Please help me find it.*

"Where did you lose it, Anne?" Eva inquired.

The spirit of Anne spoke once again: *I lost it at Joseph's mill. It fell from my hands when my dress caught in that cursed machine. I was knitting it for my unborn child...*

I've lost my husband. Why must I lose my child too? I feel it still inside me.

"Please come forward, Anne. We want to help you." But there was only silence in reply, and Eva could no longer feel Anne's presence in the room.

"She's gone," Eva told the others. "She was not ready to cross over. She cannot let go of her unborn child. Jim was right in believing that she was pregnant when he found the tiny bonnet at the mill."

"Shouldn't you try to contact her again?" Erin asked with urgency in her voice.

"No. We're done here. I've exhausted my strength. She will go in time. Perhaps someone else will be able to help her cross over. She will need to accept the fact that her unborn child died with her that tragic day at the mill before she'll be ready to leave this earth. I can't force her."

Eva was crying softly. She excused herself and went to get some water from the kitchen.

Seth was waiting anxiously there.

"I think it's over, Seth. Your wife should no longer be troubled by nightmares."

She explained to him that Erin's dreams, and possibly those of his sister, were the manifestation of the struggle between the dark presence of the murderer and the spirits of Mary and her children. "Mary won in the end. But we couldn't help Anne. She wasn't ready to cross over."

Eva gestured toward the living room. "You can go see the others now."

42

After the séance, both Cathy and Erin began to sleep peacefully. There were no more nightmares.

The images of the doll in Lloyd's videotape and Keisha's photo from the canal museum disappeared. The doll had obviously represented the one that Mary Holden's young child had since carried over with her to eternity.

The image of the young woman in the videotape of the old mill, however, still remained. As Eva had speculated, Anne was not yet ready to cross over. Both Eva Maynard and Jim Evans could confirm from experience that not all ghost stories had a happy ending.

Sarah believed that the spirit of Arthur Holden, which had probably haunted the old jail, was at peace now, having been reunited with his wife Mary and their three children. She also knew that there were many more prisoners whose stories needed to be told. But not by her. She began working as Seth's research assistant at the university and never returned to her former job as a tour guide.

Erin was able to piece the rest of the story together. She knew from the séance that the actual murderer of Robert Creighton was the false witness, Marc Jordan. Ironically, he had died ten years later in the same jail as Arthur Holden. Jordan had been imprisoned for theft when another prisoner beat him until he was unconscious. They had been arguing over a gambling debt. Jordan died of his injuries.

43

It had been a week since the séance, and Erin and Seth were both reading in their apartment when she suddenly announced, "C'mon, I need some exercise. Let's go skating on the canal before the ice melts."

They grabbed their skates and headed toward the canal. Neither of them was a good skater, but they usually managed to get around on the ice without too many spills. It helped that the temperature was very cold now, and the ice had few soft spots.

With a shiver Erin remembered the nightmare she'd had of the ice cracking and of being pulled down into the black water.

As she looked up from the surface of the ice at which she'd been staring, she saw a mother pushing her young child in a homemade sleigh. The toddler was bundled in a pink snowsuit and scarf with only her eyes visible. She was squealing with delight, waving her chubby, mittened hands back and forth in her excitement.

Erin watched the child for a few moments and then threw back her head and laughed.

It felt wonderful.

Acknowledgments

I would like to thank my husband Mike McCann for his support at every stage of this book. He not only read the draft and offered suggestions for its improvement, but also designed the covers and performed the necessary work for its publication. He did all of this in between his own writing. Thanks, Mike, for everything.

I would also like to acknowledge the debt owed to the many workers who built the Rideau Canal. It's amazing to think that it was constructed by hand with only the use of a few simple tools.

The canal museum where Erin Murphy conducts her research in this story is modelled on the Bytown Museum. I made extensive use of the very informative Bytown Museum website at http://www.bytownmuseum.com/en/index.html.

As part of the website, there is an excellent source document entitled "History of a Collection" (2011) which provides a history of the museum and its various artifacts, including the death hand of Thomas D'Arcy McGee, as well as a detailed bibliography of additional sources: http://www.bytownmuseum.com/PDF/History_of_a_collection.pdf.

Another excellent reference source I consulted is *Legacy in Stone: The Rideau Corridor* by Fiona Spalding-Smith and Barbara A. Humphreys (1999: Boston Mills Press). This book provides a photographic history of the canal and the stone buildings that remain along the Rideau Corridor. It also contains a detailed bibliography for further reference.

There are numerous sources of information on the assassination of Thomas D'Arcy McGee and the trial and execution of Patrick Whelan. For example, please see: http://www.thecanadianencyclopedia.ca/en/article/the-assassination-of-thomas-darcy-mcgee-feature/.

To go on a virtual tour of the Rideau Canal and other Ottawa locations mentioned in this novella, please visit: http://www.ottawakiosk.com/panos/virtual.html.

To learn more about early Ottawa (Bytown), please see http://en.wikipedia.org/wiki/Bytown and the related bibliography. For information on the logging trade and lumber barons, see http://en.wikipedia.org/wiki/Ottawa_River_timber_trade and the related bibliography.

For the uncovering of the Ottawa burial site referred to in this story, please see http://ottawa.ctvnews.ca/work-crews-uncover-a-historic-burial-site-in-downtown-ottawa-1.1576838.

For general information on the burial sites and cemeteries for canal workers, I have referred to http://www.rideau-info.com/canal/tales/grave-revealing.html.

For information on markers and memorials for the canal workers, see http://www.rideau-info.com/canal/history/ memorials.html.

The nature museum at which Cathy Davis works is modelled on the Canadian Museum of Nature. I am indebted to its interactive and informative website at http://nature.ca/en/home for details used in this novella.

The old jail where Sarah Bennett was once a tour guide is based on the former Carleton County Gaol, now the HI (Hostelling International)– Ottawa Jail Hostel. To learn about its history, please see: http://www.historicplaces.ca/en/rep-reg/place-lieu.aspx?id=8443.

Other reference sites related to the jail include http://www.waymarking.com/waymarks/WM2F-BY_Old_Ottawa_Jail and http://www.hihostels.ca/Ontario/1474/Ontario/HI-Ottawa-Jail/History-of-the-Jail/index.hostel.

For photographs of the old jail, please see http://www.ottawacountysheriff.org/Old Photographs/Old photo page.html. One of the sheriffs associated with the jail was Sheriff Faust. (What more proof do we need that its prisoners were consigned to hell?) For photographs of the renovations to the old Ottawa jail, please see http://www.hostelz.com/hostel/2107-HI---Ottawa-Jail-Hostel. Incidentally, the reviews of the hostel are fun to read. One of the major complaints is the lack of reliable internet service.

The old mill where Jim Evans and his paranormal team conduct their investigations is modelled on Watson's Mill in Manotick. There is information on this building in the aforementioned *Legacy in Stone: The Rideau Corridor* and online at http://www.watsonsmill.com/Home.html.

For a list of persons executed in Canada from 1860 to abolition, see http://canadaonline.about.com/cs/crime/a/cappuntimeline.htm.

For information on the hangman Arthur Ellis (pseudonym for Arthur B. English), please see

http://en.wikipedia.org/wiki/Arthur_B._English.
He presided over more than six hundred hangings.

The old song that Jim Evans refers to is "Daddy Sang Bass," written by Carl Perkins and sung by Johnny Cash. The line he is trying to remember is "[n]o, the circle won't be broken."

For the text of Oscar Wilde's "The Ballad of Redding Gaol," see http://www.poets.org/poetsorg/poem/ballad-reading-gaol.

And now to the ghosts! For paranormal investigations of the Bytown Museum and Watson's Mill, please see the Haunted Ottawa Paranormal Society website at http://hauntedottawa.net/.

For further information on the museum's haunting, please see http://www.hauntedhovel.com/bytownmuseum.html, http://www.timminspress.com/2013/10/25/history-haunted-hot-spots-abound and https://www.youtube.com/watch?v=5ZuElJLMIH0.

Among the reported signs of haunting, many of which I have adapted for this story, are museum dolls watching people with their eyes, crying and winking; walls weeping tears; visitors being shoved and poked by unseen presences; electronic equipment being tampered with; strange messages appearing on computers; and a voice yelling "Get Out". Barbara Smith in *Ontario Ghost Stories* (1998: Lone Pine Press) tells of the smoke detectors in the museum dropping their covers in unison as referenced in http://torontoghosts.org/index.php?/20080822407/Eastern-Ontario/Ottawa-Bytown-Museum.html.

It's speculated that there are at least six ghosts haunting the Bytown Museum, one of which is the ghost of a dog.

For information on the real-life Robert and Annabelle dolls, please see my blog posts on Behind the Walls of Nightmare at: http://wallsof-nightmare.blogspot.ca/2015/02/robert-haunted-doll.html and http://wallsofnightmare.blogspot.ca/2015/02/Annabelle-doll.html.

To learn more about the haunting of the Canadian Museum of Nature, please see http://www.examiner.com/article/the-canadian-muse-um-of-nature-one-of-ottawa-s-most-notorious-haunts and http://torontoghosts.org/index.php?/20080822404/Eastern-Ontario/Ottawa-The-Museum-of-Nature.html.

For tales of the haunting of Watson's Mill, see: http://www.rideau-info.com/canal/tales/ghost-watsons.html and http://www.torontoghosts.org/index.php?/20080822408/Eastern-Ontario/Man-otick-Watson-s-Mill.html.

For haunting stories of the former Ottawa jail, please see http://www.torontoghosts.org/index.php?/20080822405/Eastern-Ontario/Ottawa-Nicholas-St.-Hostel.html and http://www.toron-toghosts.org/index.php?/20080822405/Eastern-Ontario/Ottawa-Nicholas-St.-Hostel.html.

For information on other haunted sites briefly referenced in this novella, please see: http://www.torontoghosts.org/index.php?/20080822406/Eastern-Ontario/Ottawa-Chateau-Laurier.html (Fairmont Chateau Laurier); http://www.torontoghosts.org/index.php?/20091109646/Eastern-Ontario/Ottawa-Lisgar-Collegiate-Institute.html (Lisgar Collegiate Institute); and http://www.

flickr.com/photos/34537752@N02/5126825425/
in/photostream/ (Grant House). Incidentally,
Dr. Grant practised medicine at the old Carleton
County Gaol.

If you'd like to learn more about Ottawa's
haunted walk on which Sarah's tour guide respon-
sibilities are based, please see: http://www.haunt-
edwalk.com/.

For general information on paranormal investigations, I am indebted to Paranormal Studies &
Investigations Canada (PSIC) at http://psican.org/
alpha/index.php?/Paranormal-Canada/Paranor-
mal-Resources-Online/.

I would also like to acknowledge the "Ghost
Research and Investigation Course Document" by
Matthew James Didier at http://www.torontog-
hosts.org/course/coursebook.pdf, which outlines
how a paranormal investigation should be conducted. Jim Evans's objectivity and the tools he
chooses, including the laser pointer, owe much to
this document.

The provenance of the "ring around the rosie"
nursery rhyme is explained at http://www.rhymes.
org.uk/ring_around_the_rosy.htm.

One final note regarding "Circle of Souls": This
is a work of fiction. The haunted sites in this novella
have been fictionalized, as has the paranormal
society investigating the sites. And while the
story of the death of Joseph Merrill Currier's wife
Anne (spelled "Ann" or "Annie" in some reference
documents) at the Manotick mill is true, there is no
record of her pregnancy. This detail is invented for
the sake of the story.

As for the ghosts who supposedly inhabit these sites, well, who really knows?

About the Author

Lynn Clark was born in Woodstock, New Brunswick. She received her B.A. and M.A. from Acadia University in Wolfville, Nova Scotia. Prior to her retirement in 2011, she worked for the federal government in Ottawa, Ontario, Canada. She lives in a small town in eastern Ontario with her husband, crime fiction writer Michael J. McCann. She is also the author of *The Home Child*.

If you enjoyed Lynn L. Clark's
FIRE WHISPERER & CIRCLE OF SOULS
you won't want to miss

The
Home Child
a supernatural novel

*what if you
could never go
home again?*

Lynn L. Clark

CPSIA information can be obtained at www.ICGtesting.com
Printed in the USA
LVOW11s0701301115

464646LV00001B/1/P